U0165583

國際商務英語
溝通策略與運用

International Business English
Communication Strategies and Application

五南圖書出版公司 印行　　　　　　黃靜悅◎著

ENGLISH

　　臺灣的國際商務貿易處境如同本身的特殊國際地位一樣艱辛，網路興起及金融風暴後，能存活的公司必然有其能耐。唯目前臺灣國際商務貿易仍以中小企業為主，多數人事精簡，公司求才若渴，期許新人擁有各方面的優秀能力，並盡早進入狀況，但教導新人需要人力與時間，新血養成極為不易；另一方面，新人助理抱著試試看的心態，並不十分了解自己是否適合擔任國際業務。因此公司與新人彼此耽誤的情形，並非少見。

　　對於有志進入國際商務者，英語語言溝通能力與國際商務知識是基本需求，當今市面並無任何教科書或懶人包一步步教導新人如何在國際商務汪洋大海裡求生存，了解自己需要什麼樣的熱忱、知識、溝通與語言能力、敏感度與工作態度（工作不滿三年都不算經驗），才能從業務助理晉升為能獨當一面，為公司帶來獲利，為個人培養工作成就與晉級薪資的國際業務。

　　本書出版目的在於彌補以上的落差，一來減少新人養成期間瞎子摸象的階段，快速培訓業務助理了解自己的組織角色與所需具備的各項知識與英語溝通能力，二來提供國際商務貿易公司各種真實個案，所選案例客戶多為業界打滾數十年，資深老江湖等級或家族經驗傳承二代青出於藍的經理人，通常一出招就令人難以招架。本書專為拆解國際商務貿易界的疑難雜症而寫，無論是業務老手或菜鳥新人都可從本書獲得第一手破解客戶招數的溝通攻防策略。

FOREWORD 推薦序

　　今日科技發展一日千里、百家爭鳴，全球化經濟的影響帶來二十四小時不眠不休的國際市場，以機器人取代人工，無疑是我們即將面臨前所未有的挑戰。迎向未知，只有更好的思考與整合力，才能幫助我們解決問題，正如愛因斯坦所言：「教育不在於學習事實，而在於訓練人的思考。」（Education is not the learning of facts but the training of the mind to think.）

　　面對當今高等教育的嚴峻挑戰，本校各院系無不竭盡所能，培養青年學子具備結合專長領域的語言溝通力與國際移動力，並保持人文關懷與學習熱忱，增進跨領域的整合能力，擁有「走跳全球」與「行銷在地」的優勢能力，以貢獻社會。

　　然而，有志國際商務者如對職場工作一知半解，必然經歷辛苦的摸索期，也可能面臨種種問題，如頂尖國際業務究竟如何思考？處理棘手狀況有何竅門？如何與客戶使用運動術語拉近距離？如何掌握語言權？何時善用當今全球英文與中文熱，巧妙使用帶有中文特色的語言，在英文溝通過程中創造更多國際利基？

　　本校管理學院應用外語學系黃靜悅老師以多年的教學研究經驗，特別為學子編著一本融合商務與語言的實用工具書。本書「先備知識寶典」提供成為國際頂尖業務好手的寶貴知識祕笈，透過《孫子兵法》中「故上兵伐謀，其次伐交，其次伐兵，其下攻城。攻城之法，為不得已」的概念，構思了精彩的章節案例與過招的攻防回合，交互運用「謀、交、兵」之策略，集古今中外策略思考實戰，實為商務英語溝通書籍中獨樹一幟之作。附錄提供「老闆

的地雷句」與「看懂溝通招術」，為職場新人增進溝通的智慧。

　　黃老師在美國完成學業後，正巧於本人擔任教務長期間進入本校任教，多年來投入教學與著作，至今五度榮獲本校專任教師出版教學專書獎勵，數次由本人授獎，見證她努力不懈的豐碩成果。黃老師除致力寫作外，著作時時更新續版，亦參與許多國際城市之書展，並於大陸地區持續出版，嘉惠眾多學子，本人謹以此序表示敬意，也期許黃老師於教學研究之餘，繼續跨領域開發新地平線，為有意自我提升的學習者，提供更豐富充實的著作。

實踐大學　校長　陳振貴

AUTHOR'S PREFACE 作者序
國際商務新手準備好了嗎？

放眼當今國際商場難題日新月異，每人在校所學能應用到未來社會的部分可能相當有限，商務主管感嘆不但找不到可擔當大任的新人，甚至現今畢業的多數新人對書信無感，不知道客戶書信的重點在哪裡，語言程度與專業知識皆不足，工作態度欠積極，回信差錯惹怒客戶的情形，絕不少見。

但商場如戰場，多數公司精簡人力能教導新人的時間及人力有限，新人接替離職人員，必須盡快找到頭緒，才能接續工作與客戶溝通；公司期待新手必須盡快上軌道解決問題，但新手是否準備好當國際商務好手？多少新人應徵時，不了解業務工作並不是追求小確幸者的港灣，更不適合只喜好待在舒適圈的人。沒有準備好之心態與業界知識、溝通技巧、如何進入國際場域與各國如狐、狼、鷹等級之業務老手高層精英周旋鬥智，還要能出奇制勝開創業績？

對於國際客戶江湖老手的來信，如果新人讀完客戶寫來的信，卻完全「無感」，抓不到重點，讀不出脈絡跟客戶寫信目的，抓不出裡面的魔鬼細節、弦外之音（特殊英語用字），好似叢林小兔，不但解決不了問題，還會替公司製造新問題，嚴重者導致公司割地賠款，甚至因而倒閉！

在現實的商業活動中，廠商跟客人的交易互動方式有千百種，買賣雙方各有盤算，比的是實力跟服務，絕非如象牙塔中的一翻兩瞪眼，沒錢就不要買。在薄利、資訊透明與貨比三家、不景氣的時代，好客戶不會天上掉下來，碰到諸多要求、機關算盡的客戶是常態，能做到別人不能做的，並做得比別人好，「The more we do, the more we can do.」才可能保有競爭力,持續有生意上門。換句話說,賣產品之外,還要提供內容與服務。

客戶的每封信背後有其目的,交易策略、拖延付款、嫌貨比貨、翻臉索賠、要求降價等各種過招、砍價技巧,新人態度、知識能力不足,如何從客戶書信蛛絲馬跡讀出究竟客戶想要什麼?如何讀出過往交易歷史及掌握上封信、這封信以及下封信該怎麼接招、如何解讀、怎麼回覆溝通,甚至預測什麼回覆會導致什麼結果?

除了必須能夠讀出客戶信件真正的重點,新人更必須搞懂自己的角色在公司組織裡的關係,才能了解自己如何回信,見風駛帆,或有什麼武器可用,才能談得上如何使用及精進溝通技巧。這當然包括了解客戶端的組織,來往信件對方的權力層級,知己知彼,好比戲劇一般,必須了解主角與各角色與環境的關係,才能看得懂如何進行,如何接續。

除了要求自我工作能力提升之外,正因商場難題日新月異,只當白天鵝是不夠的,能扮演「天鵝湖」主角的是黑天鵝。客戶絕非省油的燈,「客大欺商」或是「商大欺客」,商場充滿詭譎多變的角力戰,端看如何角力維持平衡,才能繼續生意往來。

雙方互相角力經常比的是實力(財力、專利、技術等),客戶知道你有能耐,就能不戰而屈人之兵。因此商務溝通有時像跳舞一般,配合節奏,你進我退;有時必須像叢林野戰,比誰的武器強大,使對方乖乖就範。而無論買賣溝通問題如何包山包海,國際時局如何變化萬千,開創業績固然重要,但公司有利潤才能生存,有效的溝通一定要能把貨款收回。也就是俗語所說:「會賣東西不是師傅,會收帳才是師傅。」

諷刺的是在資本主義掛帥的時代,客戶即使有錢有名氣,並不表示客戶就願意付款或準時付款,即使是行業中的前幾名也是

如此。當今數一數二商業集團的企業目標可能在於運用各種牟利甚至不義手段，讓公司愈來愈大，而愈來愈大的企業才愈能從訂購大量產品苛扣中小企業供應商的付款條件而獲利，企業倫理或商業信譽反倒是其次。

所以國際業務老手給新人難題，讓公司吃悶虧，可說易如反掌，在商界是天經地義。叢林世界物競天擇是鐵律，小白兔如何對戰狐、狼、鷹？難怪主管感嘆「好的業務帶你上天堂，不好的業務讓老闆住病房」，但要想解決問題，甚至勝出這些資深老江湖，談何容易？

鑑於解決以上業務新人的種種問題，本書以近年來的真實國際商務貿易個案為藍本，期盼將資深國際業務經理人長久實戰累積之豐富專業知識與攻防溝通技巧，傳承給積極求知、肯做肯學，希望自己打出國際業務一片天的新世代。

每個真實案例按發展逐步解析，幫助新人看懂客戶的布局或mind game，看出客戶真正要的是什麼，新人先行思考試寫發信回信，從「教戰守則」了解如何在狀況渺茫不明的時候找出脈絡掌握頭緒，做出最好的判斷，著手破解客戶的戲法，思考戰略步驟，遠離陷阱。

從比較中學習選擇正確的策略與溝通方法，運用文字攻防角力與攻心為上，寫出神回覆，立刻扭轉局勢使客戶停止纏鬥，結束攻防。案例尚包含到國外拜訪客戶，雙方進行商務會議之前置準備，會議競合交鋒，並掌握會後會議紀錄發送話語權。以及在機不可失場合，學習運用商務社交場合之敬酒時機，利用客戶在雙方員工前保留誠信顏面，而翻轉局面化解僵局之案例。

新人如能運用本書國際商務「先備知識寶典」與英語溝通策略精髓，必能提升相當之商戰實力，從新人變專業，使主管安心賦予重任，工作更上層樓！重要的是，讀者切勿將本書對策攻防，僅作負面解釋，而應考慮合情合理的商業倫理，運籌帷幄，採取適當對策回應客戶不合理的要求，才是本書宗旨，更有甚者創造雙贏或都贏，雙方生意也才可長可久。在經濟不成長的時局裡，能幫你的老闆解決難題，做到難做的生意，那麼無論你在世界的任何角落，都是業界搶著要的國際頂尖業務高手！

　　無盡感謝國際商務貿易資深經理人好友之無私貢獻，為本書開啟撰寫初衷，實踐大學陳振貴校長慨為作序鼓勵與老師同學家人朋友們持續的支持，以及五南出版社夥伴賦予本書新樣貌順利付梓。本書如有助培養國際商務貿易新血，便是對作者最大的勉勵與回饋！

　　願與所有立志於此的讀者共勉之。

作者

黃靜悅　謹誌

特點說明 Benefits and Features of the Book

case 02 客戶因原物料降價要求降價
Client Requesting Price Reduction due to Lower Raw Material Cost

章節標題 →

臺灣LH集團 VS 美國TOP AUTO集團

客戶與案例背景說明
Background of the Client and the Case

　　美國中部的客戶，進口商與零售商（實體及網路），六十多歲，大學畢業，早年在臺灣經商，對中國大陸也熟悉，是生意上的老江湖，雙方商業往來二十多年，但客戶卻慣性拖欠貨款，愈欠愈久，拖欠貨款目的愈來愈明顯。於2008年金融危機時，連續來信數封，每封皆要求降價，並提出鐵材降價，工資等數據。

　　我方如何因應？

Round 2
第二回合

客戶來信說明訴求

客戶背景資訊及案例情境描述

客戶來信 Letter from the Client

Dear Frank,

　　Thank you for meeting me in China and bringing along the samples. It is our hope to add them to our line of products.

　　The attachment is a list of the raw materials we discussed. The prices have gone down as shown. Since the oil price has decreased, along with the reductions of the raw materilas, LH cost for Top Auto must have also become much lower. When the material costs increased, LH raised up the product price by 12%. Now the costs of the materials have gone down. LH must return Top Auto the price reduc-

既然原物料成本已經下降，LH必須配合Top Auto降價。

誠摯祝福，

亨利

解讀客戶信件中的
重點、意圖

客戶來信：重點解讀 Getting the Hidden Messages

客戶開啓戰場，來信要求降價，客人繼續來第二封信催促降價，長篇大論，所有的重點只有一個：要求降價。客人像海浪一波波，列出他認爲我們要降價的原因（最大原因是：原物料及油價下降，並且我們在原物料上漲時曾經漲過價）。

客戶丟出一個個非降價不可的理由，並且在信中再次稱呼主管名字必須降價，讀起來令人壓迫感十足。但從另一方面來看，雖然降價馬上就面臨侵蝕利潤的問題，但客戶會寫長信給我們，也是看重我們，至少把我們當作優先採購的第一順序。

▶ 語言陷阱 Language Traps:

點出客戶信件中的文字陷阱與背後目的

1. Since the oil price has decreased, along with the reductions of the raw matierlas, LH cost for Top Auto must have also become much lower.

   因爲油價已經降低，加上原物料降低，LH給Top Auto的成本一定也變得更低了。

2. When the material costs increased, LH raised up the product price by 12%.

   當原物料漲價時，LH產品漲價12%。

3. Now the costs of the materials have gone down. LH must return Top Auto the price reduction to be fair.

   現在原物料價格降低了，LH必須降價給Top Auto才公平。

● **新手任務 Your Mission:**
   如何四兩撥千斤回答降價問題？

● **試寫Now You Try: 請試寫於下方**

動手練習，試試如何寫
才能達成目標

_____

_____

_____

_____

_____

_____

_____

_____

_____

_____

_____

_____

_____

_____

_____

_____

_____

_____

（試寫後才翻頁）

教戰守則 Insider Tips

面對降價要求，不需要急著回。接受客戶要求容易，卻可能害公司虧本做白工；直接回答「No」也會直接惹惱客戶。多數利潤微薄的公司，必須懂得如何婉拒客戶的要求，或僅作微小的退讓。

第一句開宗明義說明無法降價，解釋原因，歸納結論：無法降價，結尾感謝及期待繼續合作。記住第一封回覆時不提數據，提供數據可能反而進入數據大戰，或進一步被客戶瓦解而洞悉成本。總之，第一回合回覆先簡短，寫一段就好，不要寫長，愈長愈容易被挑到問題，下封再看他如何出招。

▶ 語言祕訣 Language Tips:

1. **點出公司經營原則**

   It has always been our company policy to offer our customers the best services and the most competitive prices.
   給客人最好的服務及最具有競爭力的價格，一直都是本公司的原則。

2. **告知售價計算結果**

   After recalculating all costs again for your order, **we confirm that** the price remains unchanged.
   經過本公司的仔細計算，我們確定售價維持不變。

3. **解釋原因一**

   Although the iron price has gone down a little lately, the labor costs in production, in-land delivery, and international shipment **have rocketed in recent years**.
   雖然鐵材近來有下降一些，但生產製造的人工成本，內陸運

輸及國際運輸成本近年來一飛沖天。

4. 解釋原因二

In addition, **the increases of** the taxes and labor insurances have been imposed upon us.

此外，各種稅金及勞工保險的增加也被強加進我們的成本。

5. 要求同理心（面臨持續變動的處境）

With all kinds of costs going up drastically, **you can see what business environment we are facing** now to meet China's ever-increasing demands.

面對所有劇烈的成本上升，您可以理解我們為了配合中國不斷增加的要求，目前正面臨何種商業處境。

6. 感謝支持

We are obliged to your kind support over the years **and look forward to** your continuing business in the future.

我們不會忘記您多年來的支持，期待您將來的持續關照。

▶ 關鍵字詞 Key Words and Phrases:

competitive (adj.) 競爭力的
recalculate (v.) 重新計算
labor costs in production 生產的人工成本
in-land delivery 內陸運輸
international shipment 國際運輸
rocket (v.) 急速升高
labor insurance 勞工保險
impose (v.) 強加
ever-increasing (adj.) 不斷增加的

介紹回信必備的重點字詞

drastically (adv.) 劇烈地

demand (n.) 需求

be obliged 心懷感激的

🔵 信件範例 Sample Letter:

♞ 我方發信給客戶 Our Email to the Client

攻防信件回覆範例

Dear Mr. Henry,

It has always been our company policy to offer our customers the best services and the most competitive prices. After recalculating all costs again for your order, we confirm that the price remains unchanged. Although the iron price has gone down a little lately, the labor costs in production, in-land delivery, and international shipment have rocketed in recent years. In addition, the increases of the taxes and labor insurances have been imposed upon us. With all kinds of costs going up drastically, you can see what business environment we are facing now to meet China's ever-increasing demands. We are obliged to your kind support over the years and look forward to your continuing business in the future.

Most sincerely yours,

Frank

親愛的亨利先生：

　　給客人最好的服務及最具有競爭力的價格，一直都是本公司的原則。因此，經過本公司的仔細計算，我們確定售價維持不變。雖然鐵材近來有下降一些，但生產製造的人工成本、內陸運輸及國際運輸成

本近年來一飛沖天，此外，各種稅金及勞工保險的增加也被強加進我
們的成本。面對所有成本劇烈地上升，您可以理解我們為了配合中國
不斷增加的要求，目前正面臨何種商業處境。我們公司不會忘記您多
年來的支持，期待您將來的持續關照。

補充說明
預測與對策

　　極誠摯地，

　　法蘭克

▶ 進入第三回合之前的心理準備與策略

　　客戶會寫這麼長的信，提出一堆數據就表示後續可能會死纏爛
　　打，需要來往攻防幾回才能搞定。客戶想繼續爭取降價，就會
　　提出只利於他自己的數據，或引用競爭對手低價來殺價。當然
　　為了雙方長久利益，衡量情形，做出些微的讓步並非不可行，
　　但幅度應當僅限於些微，這部分預計可能在往返數回合後發
　　生。

Round 3
第三回合

♟ 客戶來信 Client's Letter

Mr. Frank,

　　The cost of a 20 foot container has increased in the last six
months, from $3,500 to $5,300. Top Auto is unable to pass the freight
increase to our customers. Since 2008, we have not had any opportunity to raise prices.

　　Although some of your costs have gone up, but raw material, oil,
and your currency have all gone down. We have done what you asked
to expand business with you and your business has erupted. With the

CONTENTS 目次

本書案例業主列表 A List of the Business Groups

STRATEGY

LH
集團

國際商務英語溝通：先備知識寶典
International Business Communication: A Treasury of Prior Knowledge

　　孫子云：「知己知彼，百戰不殆；不知彼而知己，一勝一負；不知彼，不知己，每戰必殆。」《孫子兵法》中，提到最多的其中一個字，就是「知」，這也跟英國作家Francis Bacon所說的「Knowledge is power.」（知識就是力量。）不謀而合。那「知」的涵義是什麼？又如何應用在我們的商業書信往來上？

　　「知」是所有策略謀劃與商務溝通的起點，也是四兩撥千斤，不戰而屈人之兵的最高境界。「知」在商業書信往來的涵義及運用上，應包括：

　　1. 你有多少決定權，

　　2. 你認為你的客戶知道你有多少決定權，

　　3. 主管，老闆對你的信任及支持度有多大，

　　簡而言之，就是你在體系地位的作用是什麼？雙方往來信件可能靈活地經由各種可能層級發出，也就是說發信人不一定是真正寫信的人。主管可能運用助理名稱發信，相對的，助理也可能用主管名義發信，但助理代寫一定要獲得主管首肯及討論，並且經主管審視後才能發信。

　　因此，一人或兩人發信，一封或兩封，所造成收信人的壓迫感，完全不同。每個人都必須知道自己在公司的角色，以及各層級的關係人，才能寫好信件，並了解如何善用郵件副本及密件，製造壓力，方式如下：

1. 利用雙方現有組織層級	• 了解各層級關係人，互相知會牽制	善用郵件副本及密件，製造壓力
2. 創造內部虛擬層級或外在單位	• 內部虛擬層級：可拖延時間並施以其他作用	例如：催款時相關人員如下： (1) 發信人：我方業務 (2) 收件人：客人、客人主管、

	• 外在單位：如信用稽察，以施壓對方還款。	我方主管 (3) 副本：我方業務助理、財務、船務
3. 最高層出馬	• 非到無法收拾，業主才出面（藏鏡人對藏鏡人）	(1) 發信人：我方老闆 (2) 收件人：客人、客人老闆、財務主管、我公司業務、我公司財務 (3) 副本：我方業務的助理

另要考慮還有當時國際情況可能如何影響雙方狀況？所以「知」有三層意思：知識、了解、智慧。

1. 跟客戶的往來信中，常遇到幾種較難處理的情況（本書章節全部包含），難處理的原因不外乎牽扯了案中案或過往交易，所以撰寫下列信件，務必跟主管充分溝通後才能寫信，斟酌語言、態度、選字，並給上司審閱後，才能發信，有了這些審慎的步驟，才不會造成後續不必要的困擾。

幾項狀況為：

(1) 出貨延遲。

(2) 買了不出貨或者急催出貨。

(3) 抱怨品質服務及包裝不良。

(4) 催付貨款。

(5) 要求降價。

(6) 改變設計，客戶不承認。

(7) 電話或會議內容，我方沒有紀錄。

2. 一個好的業務，應至少要具備下列條件：

(1) 英（外）語的溝通能力以執行以下工作。

(2) 清楚了解客人的意圖或想法。

(3) 知道如何收集背景資訊（包括客戶、產品、市場、國際局勢等資料）的途徑及方法。

(4) 知道誰是公司需要的客戶，並有能力吸引客戶上門。

(5) 能獨力齊備完整的談判條件與資料，供老闆核准及據以承諾敲下訂單。

(6) 協助同事或公司其他部門，來執行與維護訂單的順利出貨。

(7) 積極達成任務的工作心態。

3. 一個業務對於行銷的推廣要常留意到：

(1) 售前與售後的客戶服務。

(2) 市場調查以便掌握市場動態。

(3) 新舊產品的規劃與研發。

4. 一個業務應要求工廠提供的支援要有：

(1) 正確的報價（包括未來可能的變化）。

(2) 產品的規格與特性。

(3) 能提供樣品的時間，及預測樣品的完成度。

(4) 模具開發所需的時程與費用。

(5) 工廠的產能狀況。

(6) 包裝及出貨方式。

(7) 工廠對應人員的溝通能力。

5. 業務的外語能力主要用於：

(1) 書信往返。

(2) 電話應對。

(3) 從事簡報。

(4) 參加會議。

(5) 參加展覽。

(6) 客戶拜訪。

(7) 社交應酬。

6. 處理客戶投訴，最重要的工作是：

(1) 勇於面對客人。

(2) 傾聽客人的抱怨，不要跟客人爭執。

(3) 釐清問題的原因。

(4) 試圖了解客戶欲解決的方式。

(5) 請求給予時間再回覆解決的方式。

(6) 迅速與工廠聯絡，並確認問題所在。

(7) 提出我們的解決方案。

(8) 與客戶協商雙方可接受方式。

(9) 迅速將問題圓滿解決。

(10)將客訴問題及內容妥善記錄，供同事或其他部門參考。

7. 客戶投訴或產品退回的主要原因有：

(1) 無故退回。

(2) 製造瑕疵。

(3) 與客戶不良的溝通。

(4) 未按照客戶的要求執行訂單。

(5) 包裝不良導致的損壞。

(6) 消費者不當的使用。

(7) 零組件的問題。

(8) 產品內的說明書缺損、錯誤或語意不詳。

8. 要了解新的市場，下列指標要知道：

(1) 氣候。

(2) 節日。

(3) 民族與人口。

(4) 宗教。

(5) 市場分布。

(6) 歷史沿革。

(7) 政府政策。

(8) 國民所得。

(9) 社會福利。

9. 要了解新的客人，下列資料要知道：

(1) 客人的主要經營產品。

(2) 客人的銷售方式。

(3) 客人販賣該產品的歷史。

(4) 客人的採購經驗及歷史。

(5) 客人的真正想法。

(6) 客戶該次或當年欲採購量。

(7) 包裝方式。

(8) 運輸方式。

(9) 報價地點。

(10) 其他併櫃、代理，及報關資料。

10. 頂尖的業務在賣一樣產品前，至少要知道：

(1) 全球市場的胃納有多大？

(2) 市場上主要的製造商與客戶（main player）有幾個？

(3) 我們的產品特性和成本結構與競爭對手的差異。

(4) 可競爭的價格在哪裡？

(5) 我們掌握哪些核心技術？成敗的技術關鍵為何？

(6) 可能的降價空間和方式是什麼？

(7) 新產品的功能與特色。規格如何設計，與市面上現有產品的差異為何？

(8) 更新產品功能時，成本及價格是多少？開模要多久？交貨時間要多長？各種法規對於該產品的要求。

▶ 六個商業書信原則（The 6Cs of Effective Business Writing）：

1. Clarity 清楚

2. Conciseness 簡明

3. Correctness 正確

4. Concreteness 具體

5. Completeness 完整

6. Consideration/Courtesy 周到／禮貌

「Short writing makes long reading.」過於簡短的信讓收信的人必須花更多時間才能弄清楚來龍去脈，因此書信往來必須遵循以上六個基本原則，如能再具備concinnity（即內容安排協調妥當，尤其是較長的信件）以及character（品牌個性），則更為難得。

本書個案將運用以上所列要點，期許新人盡快精熟公司本身產品與各項條件，早日成為知識與溝通技巧兼備，具有專業決定權的國際業務好手。

case 01 催收客戶貨款攻防戰
Collecting Client's Overdue Payment

臺灣LH集團 VS 美國NCP集團

LH集團背景與經理人簡介（本書各案例之業主）
Background of the LH Group and the General Manager

　　LH集團為典型臺灣之中小企業，為五十多年經驗之進出口業者，歷經兩代經營與時代演進，現今公司業務部門約有三十多位員工，並於臺灣及中國設廠。客戶遍及世界，主力市場以美國、歐洲、澳洲等工業化國家為主。

　　公司業務經理Frank為臺灣國立大學機械工程與美國加州大學商業管理相關科系研究所畢，四十多歲，富產品設計研究開發及公司管理經驗，多年來LH集團已成為臺灣機具出口業之翹楚，掌握美國前三大機具進口客戶及其他市場重要客戶。近十多年來積極培養新人，對於訓練新人提攜後輩所知所學毫無保留。

客戶與案例背景說明
Background of the Client and the Case

　　合作十幾年的美國客戶，六十多歲，大學畢業，三十餘年經驗之進口商與零售商，包含實體及網路銷售，為該行業前五大的販賣商。近三年開始有推延付款的情況發生，現即將出一批五個20呎貨櫃的新貨，公司的主管要你通知客戶，付清前面積欠的貨款才願意出貨。

● 新手任務 Your Mission:

　　當主管交付催貨款任務時，你該問哪些問題，需要哪些資料來寫這封信？

● 試寫Now You Try: 請試寫於下方

_____

_____

_____

_____

_____

　　有資料後，你如何研判客戶為何不付款？怎麼催款？寫下你的想法。

_____

_____

_____

_____

_____

　　如果你不知道要找什麼資料，怎麼解讀資料？怎麼催款？有何策略技巧可用？就無法使用英（外）語溝通與表達的工具來達成目的，知識與工具兩者缺一不可。

　　思考試寫後，請翻頁，從「教戰守則」學習你需要的商務知識及策

略，從「語言祕訣」及「關鍵字詞」學習如何溝通表達的技巧。從「書信範例」學習如何運用及結合兩者達成目標。

 教戰守則 Insider Tips

你需要知道的資料可不少（見「先備知識寶典」）：

1. 客戶來往歷史
2. 客戶交易次數
3. 客戶每次交易金額
4. 客戶信用歷史狀況
5. 客戶現在人員的組織更易
6. 公司是否有調查客戶現在的財務狀況？
7. 誰可決定付款（key man）？是老闆、CFO（Chief Financial Of-ficer，財務長）、採購、倉庫主管、品管或業務？是「個人」決定還是「集體」決定？
8. 寫信及收信人是誰？
9. 最近一年內客戶是否有任何抱怨？（品質、包裝、出貨……）
10. 本公司過去收信回信人是誰？

用正式的字眼及語氣，提醒客戶付款期限已經超過。記住跟客戶的生意要繼續做下去，不要傷和氣。我們的判斷是客戶並非財務困難，卻能拖就拖，不願按時付款。因此，你必須給他足以令他無法招架的壓力，讓他立刻用付款行動解決問題，生意才能繼續做下去。

註：客戶學經歷背景是運用溝通策略絕對重要的資料，三十多年前美國人口僅10-15%大學畢業，同時期臺灣的大學錄取率為25-30%，大學生僅占同年齡人口數約8%。但臺灣自從廣設大學後學歷意義丕變，美國2015年大學畢業比例為總人口32.5%。

1. **提醒對方貨款逾期**

   你可能已經注意到訂單#1563（美金$48,550）貨款在7月15日已經到期了。

   You may have noticed that the payment of PO#1563 ($48,550) was due on Jul. 15 already.

2. **請求查詢**

   請你向財務部門確認付款狀態。

   Could you please check with your financial department about the payment status?

3. **感謝**

   感謝你的協助。

   Thank you for your assistance.

● 信件範例 Sample Letter:

♞ 我方發信給客戶 Our Email to the Client

> Dear Steve,
>
> How are you? You may have noticed that the payment of PO#1563 ($48,550) was due on Jul. 15 already, but we have not received the payment. Could you please check with your financial department about the payment status, and let us know when the payment will come in?
>
> Thank you for your assistance. If you have any questions, please inform.
>
> Best regards,
>
> Clair

親愛的史蒂夫：

　　你好，你可能已經注意到訂單#1563（美金$48,550）貨款在7月15日已經到期了，但我們還沒收到款項。可以請你跟財務部確認貨款狀況，讓我們知道何時會收到貨款嗎？

　　謝謝你的幫忙，如果有任何問題，請告知。

　　誠摯祝福，

　　克萊兒

▶ 關鍵字詞 Key Words and Phrases:

notice (v.) 注意

payment (n.) 貨款，付款

PO (purchase order) 訂單

payment status 付款狀況

assistance (n.) 協助

inform (v.) 告知，報告

客戶回信 Client's Reply (1)

Dear Clair,

　　Thanks for the message. I will get back to you soon after I check with NCP accountant about the payment status.

　　Best,

　　Steve

親愛的克萊兒：

　　謝謝你的通知，我會跟公司的會計確認付款情形後盡快回覆你。

誠摯祝福，
史蒂夫

客戶回信 Client's Reply (2)

Dear Clair,

The payment by NCP bank is set to wire transfer on 09/30/15. I'll email you the bank confirmation immediately after I receive it.

Best,

Steve

親愛的克萊兒：

NCP的銀行預計在2015年9月30日電匯貨款，我一收到銀行確認，馬上電郵給你。

誠摯祝福，

史蒂夫

 客戶來信：重點解讀 Getting the Hidden Messages

準時付款的責任在客戶，經我方通知，已屬信用不良。沒想到發出催款通知，客戶還能繼續往後推延！客戶顯然是拖延老手，發了制式回信，至少用了三個招數：首先是兩個擋箭牌（會計及銀行），再來是製造錯誤的「立即感」（見附錄二）。

客戶在第一封回覆時客戶先拿與「會計」確認當作擋箭牌拖延，第二封客戶將付款日推給「銀行」，規避責任。拖延之後，告訴你一收到銀行確認就「馬上」電郵，讓你以為看到曙光，就像魔術師身邊總是帶

著美女助理一樣，讓你分心。這時你已可判斷，從催款開始到客戶最新的承諾日（如果可靠的話），還有得熬！

▶ 語言陷阱 Language Traps:

1. I will get back to you soon after I check with NCP accountant about the payment status.

   我會跟公司的會計確認付款情形後盡快回覆你。

2. The payment by NCP bank is set to wire transfer on 09/30/15.

   NCP的銀行預計在2015年9月30日電匯貨款。

3. I'll email you the bank confirmation immediately after I receive it.

   我一收到銀行確認，馬上電郵給你。

▶ 技法字詞 Tricky Words and Phrases:

get back to you soon after ……後，立即回覆

accountant (n.) 會計

wire transfer (v.) 電匯

bank confirmation 銀行確認

Round 2
第二回合

💬 新手任務 Your Mission:

你該怎麼回覆不讓主管跳腳？能讓客戶拖下去嗎？這封郵件藏著什麼魔鬼？如何破解扳回一城？

（試寫後才翻頁）

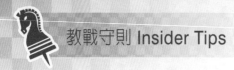

　　小心掌握及時性，不要因為這封典型的拖延信，就被客人拖掉時間。通常在發出第一封催款信的兩天後，就要發第二封催款信。

　　下一封信你應該要求客戶什麼才不會過火？如果你的用詞軟弱，客戶只會不痛不癢能拖就拖。所以你的回信必須口氣堅定，不拖泥帶水，日期、訂單、金額數字完整，句句到位。

▶ **語言祕訣Language Tips:**

1. 在感謝中提出要求

We would appreciate your on-schedule total payment of both orders US$75,688.30 on 09/30/2015.

我們感謝你將在2015年9月30日如期把兩筆訂單全數貨款美金$75,688.30付清。

2. 解釋原因

We are responsible for submitting our financial report for credit check of a **client's** financial status.

我們必須負責交出我們的財務報告，提供客戶的財務狀況做信用檢查。

3. 提出為雙方著想的作法

For this reason, your on-time payment will absolutely **do both of us good**.

因此，你們的準時付款，對我們雙方絕對是好的。

信件範例 Sample Letter:

我方發信給客戶 Our Email to the Client

Dear Steve,

Thank you for the reply about the payment of PO#1563 wire transfer on 09/30/2015.

You may have also noticed that the payment of PO#1545, 2nd shipment is already overdue (due: 08/30/2015). We would appreciate your on-schedule total payment of both orders US$75,688.30 (PO#1563: $48,550 + PO#1545 2nd: $27,138.30) on 09/30/2015.

In order to meet China Government Export Credit regulation, we are responsible for submitting our financial report (our sales contract states net 60 days after shipment) for credit check of a client's financial status. For this reason, your on-time payment will absolutely do both of us good.

Best,

Clair

親愛的史蒂夫：

謝謝你關於訂單#1563將於2015年9月30日電匯的回覆。

你可能也注意到訂單#1545第二批出貨的貨款已經逾期（2015年8月30日到期）。我們感謝你將在2015年9月30日如期把兩筆訂單全數貨款美金$75,688.30付清（PO#1563: $48,550 + PO#1545 2nd: $27,138.30）

為了要符合中國政府的出口信用規定，我們必須負責交出我們的財務報告（根據我們的合約是出貨淨60天後）供其信用檢查客戶的財

務狀況。因此，你們的準時付款，對我們雙方絕對是好的。

誠摯祝福，

克萊兒

▶ **關鍵字詞** Key Words and Phrases:

on-schedule (adj.) 準時的

meet (v.) 符合

responsible (adj.) 負責的

submit (v.) 呈交

credit check 信用檢查

financial status 財務狀況

do good 有好處

客戶無回應

Round 3
第三回合

● **新手任務 Your Mission:**

上封信給客人後，接近十天客戶都沒給你隻字片語，對你的要求不理不睬，你會怎麼做？

● **試寫Now You Try:** 請試寫於下方

（試寫後才翻頁）

教戰守則 Insider Tips

不管客戶想法怎樣,重點是要讓他回信,才能知道葫蘆裡賣什麼藥。

▶ **語言祕訣 Language Tips:**

只需一句話讓客戶回信就夠了。

詢問進展

有任何消息嗎?

Any **update**?

▶ **關鍵字詞 Key Words and Phrases:**

update (n.) 更新,最新消息

▶ **此時可撥第一通電話**

電話也是武器,財務主管通常不會說寫英文,如果主管要你打催款電話,你該怎麼說?

提醒電話第一回內容可為:

1. 客戶是否收到信?

2. 客戶是否通知財務或主管付款?

3. 何時我們可以得到回答?

信件範例 Sample Letter:

我方發信給客戶 Our Email to the Client

Dear Steve,

    Any update? Thanks.

    Best,

    Clair

親愛的史蒂夫：

    有任何消息嗎？謝謝！

    誠摯祝福，

    克萊兒

客戶回信 Client's Reply

Dear Clair,

    Thanks for the email. The follow ups of the payment status and the details from NCP accountant will be sent to you tomorrow (10/03).

    NCP has taken in the labor costs by ourselves for many years, without charging LH Group for any amount for fixing damages and quality problems. LH Group has built a good business relationship with NCP and has started inspecting and fixing goods before shipment. We appreciate your consideration to keep up the quality after the production process.

    Best regards,

    Steve

親愛的克萊兒：

謝謝你的郵件，NCP會計的付款情形與後續細節我明天（10月3日）會寄給你。

NCP多年來都自行吸收成本，沒有跟LH集團收取任何修理損害品或品質問題的金額。LH集團與NCP已經建立良好的商業關係，並且開始在出貨前檢查跟修理產品。我們感謝你們在生產過程後為了維持品質的體貼作為。

誠摯祝福，

史蒂夫

 客戶來信：重點解讀 Getting the Hidden Messages

解讀客戶回信時要思考幾件事：客戶選擇回應或不回應什麼？客戶選擇的回應如何解讀？不回應代表什麼？是否有暗示或沒說出口的重點？

客戶回信了，但使用慣用手法，外加：

客戶再度說會計師會進行處理後（擋箭牌，不知是否真的有在進行），日期又往後拖了幾天（拖延術），並且開始抱怨你公司的品質不良（以煙幕彈擾亂重點），讓他們要花很多成本修理，這是客戶在留伏筆，將來可能以這個名義扣錢，那我們要收回貨款就更困難了。雖然在信尾客戶表示感謝我們的體貼作為（裹糖衣），但那僅是表面功夫。整封信從頭到尾完全沒有回應或允諾於9月30日支付兩筆逾期款。這封信背後的意義就是「不付錢！」、「再說！」。

▶ 語言陷阱 Language Traps:

1. The follow ups of the payment status and the details from NCP

accountant will be sent to you tomorrow (10/03).

NCP會計的付款情形與後續細節我明天（10月3日）會寄給你。

2. NCP has taken in the labor costs by ourselves for many years, without charging LH Group for any amount for fixing damages and quality problems.

NCP多年來都自行吸收成本，沒有跟LH集團收取任何修理損害品或品質問題的金額。

3. We appreciate your consideration to keep up the quality after the production process.

我們感謝你們在生產過程後爲了維持品質的體貼作爲。

▶ **技法字詞** Tricky Words and Phrases:

take in 吸收

charge (v.) 索價

consideration (n.) 體貼

● 新手任務 Your Mission:

　　接下來你會怎麼做？如果攻防到第三回合，你知道這客戶還會繼續賴下去，你寫不下去想放棄了，建議你調整心態或趁早改行。別人做不下去，而你能找出辦法繼續第四回合，恭喜你！你可能適合這一行。

● 試寫Now You Try: 請試寫於下方

（試寫後才翻頁）

教戰守則 Insider Tips

先感謝客戶不會跟我們收取修理費（這是我們先定調假設，先說先贏，但還是繼續要跟客戶收錢）。回信重點須表達我方對於客戶想法與作法之感激，強調我方極度的耐性與無奈，以及雙方因此造成的損失。

▶ 語言祕訣 Language Tips:

1. **感謝對方的肯定**

   我們感謝你肯定我們是良好商業夥伴的觀點，而不向我們收取任何人力成本。

   We appreciate your perspective about our good business partnership and zero charges for any labor cost.

2. **強調我們的耐心**

   我們總是有耐心的對待你們的逾期款，即使已經超過一個多月了。

   We have been everlastingly **patient to** your overdue payment even though it has been over one month late.

3. **表達因逾期款所造成我們的困難與犧牲**

   我們的現金流動已經很困難，並且我們兩造公司的名聲已在「中國政府出口信用表現」裡受到犧牲。

   Our cash flow has suffered and both of us are **sacrificing our company reputation** for China Government Export Credit performance.

▶ 關鍵字詞 Key Words and Phrases:

perspective (n.) 看法，觀點

everlastingly (adv.) 永久地

cash flow 現金流

suffer (v.) 遭受損害

sacrifice (v.) 犧牲

reputation (n.) 名譽

● 信件範例 Sample Letter:

🔖 我方發信給客戶 Our Email to the Client

Dear Steve,

We appreciate your perspective about our good business partnership and zero charges for any labor cost. Likewise, we have been everlastingly patient to your overdue payment even though it has been over one month late. Our cash flow has suffered and both of us are sacrificing our company reputation for China Government Export Credit performance.

Best,

Clair

親愛的史蒂夫：

我們感謝你肯定我們是良好商業夥伴的觀點，而不向我們收取任何人力成本。同樣的，我們總是有耐心的對待你們的逾期款，即使已經超過一個多月了。我們的現金流動已經很困難，並且我們兩造公司的名聲已在「中國政府出口信用表現」裡受到犧牲。

誠摯祝福，

克萊兒

客戶回信 Client's Reply

Dear Clair,

Our mutual understanding certainly upgrades cooperation, as we both agreed in our last mail. NCP does best in helping LH product matters, while LH helps NCP with payment dates.

NCP's wire transfer is scheduled on 10/10. The bank confirmation will be sent to you afterwards.

Best,

Steve

親愛的克萊兒：

如同我們上封郵件所言，我們彼此的理解確實增進我們的合作，NCP盡最大努力幫助LH的產品問題，LH幫忙NCP付款日期。

NCP電匯排在10月10日，銀行確認會在之後寄給你。

誠摯祝福，

史蒂夫

 客戶來信：重點解讀 Getting the Hidden Messages

客戶又把話題繞回去了，說彼此有「共識」，在貨品及付款上彼此「合作」、「幫忙」，然後再把日期拖延到10月10日才會付錢，但前面過期的貨款何時付款，完全沒提。

▶ 語言陷阱 Language Traps:

1. Our mutual understanding certainly upgrades cooperation.

我們彼此的理解增進我們的合作。

2. NCP does best in helping LH product matters, while LH helps NCP with payment dates.

NCP盡最大努力幫助LH的產品問題，LH幫忙NCP付款日期。

3. NCP's wire transfer is scheduled on 10/10. The bank confirmation will be sent to you afterwards.

NCP電匯排在10月10日，銀行確認會在之後寄給你。

▶ 技法字詞 Tricky Words and Phrases:

mutual understanding 互相了解，共識

upgrade (v.) 增進，提升

Round 5
第五回合

🔵 新手任務 Your Mission:

客戶顯然對於你的催促，不痛不癢。你該怎麼回？

🔵 試寫Now You Try: 請試寫於下方

_____

_____

_____

_____

_____

_____

（試寫後才翻頁）

教戰守則 Insider Tips

繼續要對方付款，要破解對方繞圈圈的戰術，一開始要求對方釐清付款安排，並告知拖延再三，已使其信譽受損。最後要附上清楚的日期及兩筆逾期款清單。

▶ **此時可撥第二通電話，內容為**

1. 重複信件內容，未付款對公司影響很大。
2. 要對方告知哪一段期間（而非某一固定天）付錢，因為必須先往上呈報。
3. 告知客戶如超過期限付款，對雙方有很大損傷，恐怕以後不能再以O/A（記帳）方式作為付款條件。（第三點有關付款條件必須在電話提，不要在信裡寫，因白紙黑字寫給對方等同向客戶宣戰）。

▶ **語言祕訣 Language Tips:**

1. **要求對方說明**

   Please be clear about your arrangement for payment.
   請清楚說明付款安排。

2. **警告嚴重性**

   You have already sabotaged your credibility for these changes. **No more changes will be accepted.**
   你這些改變已經嚴重破壞你的信用。任何改變我們都不能接受。

3. **附上逾期款清單**

   The updated payment statement **is attached to show** that there

have been two delayed payments.
附上最新的付款單顯示有兩筆逾期帳款。

4. **釐清非我雙方的問題與付款無關**

   Any agreement between you and your customer's payment term **has nothing to do with our contract.**
   任何你公司與你顧客之間的付款條件與我公司的契約無關。

5. **要求對方遵守合約付款**

   LH has each contract with NCP. We delivered the goods on time, so NCP **should pay on time**!
   LH與NCP有每份合約。我們按時出貨,所以NCP理當準時付款!

▶ **關鍵字詞 Key Words and Phrases:**

sabotage (v.) 破壞

credibility (n.) 信用

updated (adj.) 更新的

payment term 付款條件

contract (n.) 合約

信件範例 Sample Letter:

我方回信 Our Email to the Client

Dear Steve,

Please be clear about your arrangement for payment. In the meantime, the delayed payment date 10/10 is unbelievable-it was due 07/15 and has been promised 08/15, and then changed to 09/30, then

10/03, and now 10/10. You have already sabotaged your credibility for these changes. No more changes will be accepted.

The updated payment statement is attached to show that there have been two delayed payments. Any agreement between you and your customer's payment term has nothing to do with our contract-LH has each contract with NCP. We delivered the goods on time, so NCP should pay on time! It is clear and simple! Thank you!

Clair

親愛的史蒂夫：

請清楚說明付款安排，同時，你拖延付款日為10月10日，實在令人無法置信，到期日為7月15日，先是承諾8月15日，然後改到9月30日，又改為10月3日，現在變成10月10日。你這些改變已經嚴重破壞你的信用。任何改變我們都不能接受。

附上最新的付款單顯示有兩筆逾期帳款，任何你公司與你顧客之間的付款條件與我公司的契約無關——LH與NCP有每份合約。我們按時出貨，所以NCP理當準時付款！就是這麼清楚簡單！謝謝！

克萊兒

客戶未回信

▶ 此時可撥第三通電話，由主管級人員撥出。

● 新手任務 Your Mission:

又過了一個星期，客戶還是無音訊！你該怎麼辦？已經到了第六回合，怎樣的信件才會讓客戶有感馬上付款？

▶ 主管可再次撥電話。

● 試寫Now You Try: 請試寫於下方

（試寫後才翻頁）

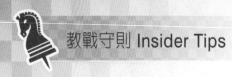

教戰守則 Insider Tips

怎樣的信件才會讓客戶有感馬上付款？答案一定要能撼動到他！以「命運共同體」的概念催促立即付款，我方必須付員工薪水以維持公司營運，否則現在就無法準時出貨給他（這是客戶真正在意的），也就沒有將來的生意跟服務了。

雙方往來信件可能靈活地經由各種可能層級發出，也就是說發信人不一定是真正寫信的人（見「先備知識寶典」）。主管可能運用助理名稱發信，相對的，助理也可能用主管名義發信，但助理代寫一定要獲得主管首肯及討論，並且經主管審視後才能發信。

因此，一人或兩人發信，一封或兩封，所造成收信人的壓迫感，完全不同。每個人都必須知道自己在公司的角色，以及各層級的關係人，才能寫好信件，並了解如何善用郵件副本及密件，製造壓力，方式如下：

1. 利用雙方現有組織層級	• 了解各層級關係人，互相知會牽制	善用郵件副本及密件，製造壓力
2. 創造內部虛擬層級或外在單位	• 內部虛擬層級：可拖延時間並施以其他作用 • 外在單位：如信用稽察，以施壓對方還款。	例如：催款時相關人員如下： (1) 發信人：我方業務 (2) 收件人：客人、客人主管、我方主管 (3) 副本：我方業務助理、財務、船務
3. 最高層出馬	• 非到無法收拾，業主才出面（藏鏡人對藏鏡人）	(1) 發信人：我方老闆 (2) 收件人：客人、客人老闆、財務主管、我公司業務、我公司財務 (3) 副本：我方業務的助理

▶ 語言祕訣 Language Tips:

強調「今天」就匯款

1. **要求立即行動**

    Please remit the two delayed payments **today to keep your word**.

    請今天就匯款支付兩筆逾期帳款以保持你的信用。

2. **要求同理心，付款行動關乎公司存亡**

    We must have the money to pay our staff salary **to keep our company working**!

    我們需要這些款項來支付員工薪水，讓公司繼續營運！

3. **告知無付款，將發生客戶最不願意見到的結果**

    Without the payment, we will not be able to ship your prod-ucts on time.

    沒收到貨款，我們將無法準時出你的貨。

▶ 關鍵字詞 Key Words and Phrases:

remit (v.) 匯款

keep your word 保持你的信用

salary (n.) 薪水

keep our company working 讓公司繼續營運

♟ 我方回信 Our Email to the Client

Dear Steve,

Please remit the two delayed payments today to keep your word. We must have the money to pay our staff salary to keep our company working! Without the payment, we will not be able to ship your products on time.

Thank you.

Clair

親愛的史蒂夫：

請今天就匯款支付兩筆逾期帳款以保持你的信用，我們需要這些款項來支付員工薪水，讓公司繼續營運！沒收到貨款，我們將無法準時出你的貨。

謝謝。

克萊兒

♟ 客戶回信 Client's Reply

1	Dear Frank and Clair,
2	Your last mail seemed a threatening letter. NCP has been pay-
3	ing LH much later than 60 days in our entire business history.
4	In our letters over the years, NCP has requested LH to over-
5	come quality problems before shipment, but quality issues happen
6	consistently after receiving products. Still the defectives have not

7   been fixed by LH. Because NCP has to inspect, test, and repair the

8   products before shipping to our customers, NCP has been forced to as-

9   sign a team responsible for solving all these problems for each piece of

10   goods, from every shipment. Despite that we have reported the same

11   problems over and over--bent rims, defective grips, locking problems,

12   poor paint jobs, etc., the defective rate remains constantly 10-15%!

13   Mark has explained kindly in earlier mails to LH that NCP has

14   covered all shipping costs, inbound and outbound, for defective

15   products, all defective claims and shipping expenses from the cus-

16   tomers, and all NCP labor costs for handling and fixing LH defec-

17   tives. In each report NCP has requested better quality control during

18   production, LH has also agreed to fix problems before shipment, but

19   NCP has been receiving from LH repeatedly the same defects!

20   NCP could pay LH within a short period of time after 60 days

21   if LH did not have constant quality problems each time. Even

22   though NCP has always strived to pay LH early, NCP has paid LH

23   much later than 60 days, usually 90 days, in our business history.

24   LH has cost NCP to inspect, test, and fix continual defects. If LH

25   could provide all quality goods, NCP would be able to make pay-

26   ment as close to 60 days as possible.

27   If LH tries to change payment dates that we have done in the

28   past, then LH has to compensate NCP's all costs for labor, ship-

29   ping, and expenses due to receiving defectives on LH shipments.

30   In the past years, NCP has cooperated with LH on dealing with

31   the defect costs, and LH cooperated with NCP on longer payment

32   dates. It has been the way that we both sides work together entirely

33   and have mutual understanding. However, if LH starts to ask for early

34	payment, then NCP must ask for reimbursement for fixing defec-
35	tives. For the constant defect rate on LH goods, the labor cost for just
36	one NCP worker to inspect, test, and fix LH defectives costs at least
37	$35,000 per year, not to mention the extra expenses for shipment (in-
38	bound and outbound, returning shipment), defective claims, etc.
39	We were about to pay for the invoice next week before receiving
40	your email to inform us that LH would not make the next shipment.
41	NCP can change our business relationship for the future, if LH
42	demands 60 days. Consequently, LH would be hurt, perhaps worse
43	than NCP's cash flow. NCP could manage to pay at 60 days every
44	time, if NCP started to bill LH all expenses to repair the defectives.
45	**In every single box, there are always some defective products!**
46	Thank you for working our business history together. If you
47	want to change our future expectations, please inform.
48	Best regards,
49	Steve

親愛的法蘭克跟克萊兒：

你的上封信看起來是個威脅信，在我們整個交易的往來歷史，NCP一向都超過60天以上才付款。

過去的幾年我們的信件裡，NCP一直要求LH在裝運前解決品質問題，但品質問題不斷地發生，到現在LH還沒有修復瑕疵品。因為NCP在運送給我們的客戶前，必須檢查、測試及修復這些產品，所以NCP被迫必須成立團隊從每一批出貨負責一個個修復這些問題。儘管我們再三報告同樣的問題——彎曲的邊緣，瑕疵的鉗夾，上鎖的問題，品質不佳的漆工等等，瑕疵品所占比率經常維持在10-15%！

馬克在先前給LH的郵件裡很好心地解釋NCP支付所有瑕疵品的

運輸成本，包含國內及國外，所有顧客的瑕疵品求償及運輸費用，以及NCP所有處理和修理LH瑕疵品的人力成本。在每份報告裡，NCP要求更好的生產過程品管，LH也同意在裝運前就修理問題。但是NCP仍然重複地收到LH同樣的瑕疵問題。

NCP可以在60天後早點付給LH，如果LH不會每次都有經常品質出錯的問題。即使NCP每次都想早點付LH貨款，但在我們的交易紀錄裡，NCP總是在60天後才付，通常是90天。因為LH讓NCP花錢在檢查、測試及不斷修理瑕疵品。如果LH可以提供完好品質的貨品，NCP就可以在60天後早早付款。

如果LH想改變我們一直以來的付款日期，那麼LH就必須賠償我們因為收到LH瑕疵品所造成的人力、運輸成本，以及所有的花費。

過去的幾年裡，NCP幫忙LH在處理瑕疵品成本上合作，而LH給予NCP較長的付款期。我們雙方一直這樣合作，並且有共識。但是如果LH開始要求早點付款，那NCP就必須要求修理賠償。因為LH持續的不良率，NCP光是一個員工人力成本去檢查、測試跟修理LH瑕疵品，每年至少就要$35,000，其他運輸費用（國內外運輸、退貨運費），瑕疵賠償等等，都還沒算進去。

在收到你的郵件通知我們不出貨之前，我們原本打算下星期就要支付發票金額。

如果LH要求60天付款，NCP可以在未來改變我們的商業關係。結果LH必然會受傷，可能傷得比NCP的現金流還嚴重。如果NCP開始開給LH帳單去支付所有的修理瑕疵品費用，NCP可以每次都做到在60天付款。**每一箱貨品內，永遠都有瑕疵品！**

感謝你與我們共同有過的交易歷史，如果你要改變我們將來的期望，請告知。

誠摯祝福，

史蒂夫

客戶來信：重點解讀 Getting the Hidden Messages

　　請客戶準時付過期款保住商譽，他說你在威脅他（注意他回信給Clair及她的主管Frank），其實客戶回信威脅意味濃厚，不要被嚇到，記住我們的目的是要客戶付款。

　　你或許認為不要跟這種客戶來往就好了，何必自找麻煩？要知道名字響叮噹的大公司付款可不見得會比較爽快，有錢的公司也不一定會願意準時付款，商界本來就是叢林，強者為王。現今的大公司可不像古早時代，把商譽誠信當生命，而是利潤至上，想辦法從供應商及其他各種可能去苛扣支出，或貪賺早該付給供應商貨款的利息，變成自己的利潤。

　　這麼長的信，要耐性仔細看完，真不簡單，偏偏你不能不仔細看完，不會有人幫你解釋或翻譯，或幫你畫重點提示你哪裡要注意，哪裡有陷阱。如果沒有耐性看完這種長度的英文，理解脈絡，或只想利用類似google翻譯等軟體，以為這樣就可以理解客人信件內容者，那麼在這一關新手要考慮趁早改行，或許你並不適合這一行。用翻譯軟體只會落得意思天差地遠，誤會大了。

　　其實客戶只講一個重點，卻不斷重複數落我方品質，讓你沉不住氣（那可能就是他的策略），更可怕的是客戶玩文字遊戲，說雙方有「共識」，意謂我方「同意」被拖延欠款，緊咬我方品質有問題（客戶拋出煙幕彈），害他要派人手檢查修理及處理後續，讓他不能在六十天付款。不斷繞圈圈後（光是defect瑕疵／defective瑕疵品就出現了將近二十次），最後丟出「你要玩，我就陪你玩」的威脅，並斬釘截鐵說我公司將會比他公司傷得更重。（見附錄二）

　　從這封信可看出客戶的老謀深算及使用的伎倆：兜圈圈，讓你開始煩，感覺混亂。再者，因為你煩了就失去該有的戒心，他正好繼續埋地雷，將拖延付款變成我們的錯，要注意他是否順序亂湊，似是而非。如

果忽略任何一顆被埋下的地雷（例如：每個員工每年花$35,000人力處理瑕疵），將來可能就被炸得體無完膚。

任何一個有英語知識的人都知道寫英文書信的邏輯不該這樣繞圈圈，但客戶可能「好心的」告訴你，他寫這麼長是因為英文不是臺灣的母語，「為你著想」，他要解釋得很清楚。事實上，不走邏輯大道，而故意繞路兜圈正是他用來對付你的武器。

針對這種客戶的對策，就是看穿他的把戲後，務必把不符事實及對我方不利的文字一個個標出及按照邏輯順序重整。標完之後，思考下一封信必須聚焦哪個問題。

▶ **語言陷阱 Language Traps:**
你看得出什麼陷阱呢？先找找看。

Line 12
The defective rate remains constantly 10-15%!
瑕疵品所占比率經常維持在10-15%!

Line 21-23
Even though NCP has always strived to pay LH early, NCP has paid LH much later than 60 days, usually 90 days, in our business history.
即使NCP每次都想早點付LH貨款，結果在我們的交易紀錄裡，NCP總是在60天後才付，通常是90天。

Line 24-26
If LH could provide all quality goods, NCP would be able to make payment as close to 60 days as possible.
如果LH可以提供完好品質的貨品，NCP就可以在60天後早早付款。

Line 30-33

In the past years, NCP has cooperated with LH on dealing with the defect costs, and LH cooperated with NCP on longer payment dates. It has been the way that we both sides work together entirely and have mutual understanding.

過去的幾年裡，NCP幫忙LH在處理瑕疵品成本上合作，而LH給予NCP較長的付款期。我們雙方一直這樣合作，並且有共識。

Line 35-38

For the constant defect rate on LH goods, the labor cost for just one NCP worker to inspect, test, and fix LH defectives costs at least $35,000 per year, not to mention the extra expenses for shipment (inbound and outbound, returning shipment), defective claims, etc.

因為LH持續的不良率，NCP光是一個員工人力成本去檢查、測試跟修理LH瑕疵品，每年至少就要$35,000，其他運輸費用（國內外運輸、退貨運費），瑕疵賠償等等，都還沒算進去。

特別注意最後兩個陷阱！

▶ **技法字詞 Tricky Words and Phrases:**
客戶使用不同詞性的同義字兜圈轟炸

1. consistently (adv.) 經常地　repeatedly (adv.) 重複地　remain (v.) 仍然　continual (adj.) 連續的

2. defective (adj.) 瑕疵的　defectives (n.) 瑕疵品　defect/defective rate 不良率／瑕疵品比率　defective claims 瑕疵賠償 defect (n.) 瑕疵，缺陷

3. assign a team responsible for... 專門派一團隊負責……

4. strive (v.) 努力，苦幹

5. mutual understanding 共識

6. compensate (v.) 賠償　reimbursement (n.) 彌補　bill (v.) 開帳單

Round 7
第七回合

🔵 新手任務 Your Mission:
面對打混戰的客戶，你該怎麼辦？

🔵 試寫Now You Try: 請試寫於下方

（試寫後才翻頁）

教戰守則 Insider Tips

回信時先避開品質的問題，才不會掉入客人的混戰中。

開頭先說明討論是有原則的，也要強調雙方情誼，但我方因無利潤又頻頻遭遇對方推拖欠款（貼上附件清單、清楚證據），產生現金流困難，所以對方必須信守合約日期付款。接下來就看客戶是否要選擇配合付款日期，我方扮演黑白臉，給予蘿蔔（贈信用額度）或棍棒（停止出貨）。

因為日期很重要，每個過年後要把今年節日（臺灣、中國）放假日給客戶，並且跟客戶要（美國的）行事曆。注意我方催款信件要指出B/L day（提單日）而不是ETD（Estimated Time of Departure，預計開航時間），因為貨物早就出去了。

另外，我方需檢查PI（proforma invoice）付款條件是否精準記載（T/T WITHIN 60 DAYS AFTER B/L DATE）避免使用「after 60 days」的付款條件，因「after」指的並非固定時間點，反給客戶拖延付款可乘之機。付款條件應直接載明付款日期，也就是我方要算好幾月幾日之前（即60天內付款）客戶必須付款，並加註如何處理逾期付款之罰則。

▶ **語言祕訣 Language Tips:**

1. **建議討論的原則（對方不應有藉口）**
   We hope to have a **rational, operative, trustworthy discussion** that is based on our long term business relationship.
   我希望我們相互的討論是理性的、可執行的、守信用的，並互相珍惜長期以來的商業情誼。

2. **表達對方造成之困難**
   We are facing a severe cash flow challenge, especially before

Chinese New Year.

本公司現在面臨很嚴峻的現金流的挑戰，尤其是中國新年前。

3. **指出對方已享有價格優勢**

We have offered you a cut-throat nearly non-profit price.

我們給你的價格幾乎就是我們沒有利潤的成本價格。

4. **要求遵守協定**

By all means you must follow our order payment agreement.

請你務必遵守雙方的付款協定。

5. **提供誘因**

When the payment is received, **your company will be awarded** $50,000 line of credit.

收到貨款後，貴公司將獲得$50,000美金的信用額度。

6. **說明逾期付款後果**

When overdue payment exceeds $50,000, **we will stop shipping** any products.

若超過$50,000美金的未付款，或發生貨款過期未付，我們就停止出貨。

7. **再次要求付清欠款**

Clear out remaining and overdue payments in 2015 to balance our company finance.

付清2015年的貨款使本公司財務平衡。

8. **重申唯一解決之道**

Only when the payments are received will our Financial Department agree to continue shipment.

只有付清貨款，本公司的財務部門才會同意繼續出貨。

▶ **關鍵字詞 Key Words and Phrases:**

rational (adj.) 理性的

operative (adj.) 可執行的

trustworthy (adj.) 守信用的

cut-throat (adj.) 割喉的

award (v.) 授予

line of credit 信用額度

● **信件範例 Sample Letter:**

♞ 我方發信給客戶 Our Email to the Client

Dear Steve and Mark,

In fact, your company has long overdue payment more than 100 days, not 60 or 90 days you mentioned in your letter.

Such as

1. PO#1545 (1st) B/L day 3/20

   Payment Received: 7/30

   (breaking contract agreement)

2. PO#1557 B/L day 4/10

   Payment Received: 8/20

   (breaking contract agreement)

3. PO#1563 B/L day 5/15

   Today 09/05 still unpaid

   (breaking contract agreement)

4. PO#1545 (2nd) B/L day 6/30

   Due Date: 8/30

   (unpaid, breaking contract agreement)

We hope to have a rational, operative, trustworthy discussion that is based on our long term business relationship. We are facing a severe cash flow challenge, especially before Chinese New Year. To make matters worse, we have offered you a cut-throat nearly non-profit price. By all means you must follow our order payment agreement.

1. Make on-time payment, T/T within 60 days after B/L day, according to your order (Ref. attachment PO#1563). When the payment is received, your company will be awarded $50,000 line of credit. When overdue payment exceeds $50,000, we will stop shipping any products.

2. Clear out remaining and overdue payments in 2015 to balance our company finance. Only when the payments are received (Ref. attachment 20151215 Statement) will our Financial Department agree to continue shipment.

Thank you!

Clair

親愛的史蒂夫跟馬克：

事實上現在貴公司的付款早已超過100天，並非如你信中所說的60天或90天。

例如：

1. PO#1545第一批貨提單日 3/20　收款日7/30（違反合約）

2. PO#1557提單日　　　　 4/10　收款日8/20（違反合約）

3. PO#1563提單日　　　　5/15　今日09/05尚未收到貨款（違反合約）

4. PO#1545第二批提單日 6/30　到期日8/30（尚未收到貨款，違反合約）

我希望我們相互的討論是理性的、可執行的、守信用的，並互相珍惜過去這麼多年來的合作歷史。本公司現在面臨很嚴峻的現金流的挑戰，尤其是中國新年前，再加上我們給你的價格幾乎就是我們沒有利潤的成本價格，所以請你務必遵守雙方的付款條件。

1. 請遵守貴公司的合約，付款條件是提單日後60天內電匯（參考附件PO#1563），收到貨款後，貴公司將獲得$50,000美金的信用額度，若超過$50,000美金的未付款，或發生貨款過期未付，我們就停止出貨。

2. 請盡快付清2015年的貨款（參照20151215清單）使本公司財務平衡，只有付清貨款，本公司的財務部門才會同意繼續出貨。

謝謝！

克萊兒

客戶回信 Client's Reply

Dear Clair,

We have already explained NCP costs and cash flow due to receiving defectives from LH Group, but it seems we have got the same response from your reply. We will not continue the discussion in this mail.

One correction has to be made about the due date in your last mail: PO#1563 was received on Jul. 7. The due date at 60 days for PO#1563 is Sep. 7, which is still 2 days ahead.

Please let us know the answer to this question at your earliest convenience: if NCP pays LH PO#1563 next week, will LH ship #1576 immediately?

Best Regards,

Steve

親愛的克萊兒：

我們已經解釋了因為收到LH集團的瑕疵品，而產生NCP成本跟現金流問題，但我們好像收到你們一樣的回覆，在這封信裡我們不再繼續談這個問題了。

你上封信裡的到期日有個錯誤要更正，PO#1563收貨日是7月7日，60天到期日是9月7日，離今天9月5日還有2天。

請盡早讓我知道這個問題的答案：如果NCP下週付LH PO#1563的貨款，LH是否馬上出PO#1576的貨？

誠摯祝福，

史蒂夫

 客戶來信：重點解讀 Getting the Hidden Messages

客戶依然指責我們貨品瑕疵，但態度有些軟化，願意再付一批貨款，支付拖延的過期款，雙方溝通終於出現轉機。然而，我們還是要讓客戶了解我方也有現金流壓力，即使貨款不多，我方必須支付出去的錢就要支付出去，所以客戶該付款給我們的時間就要按日期付，我們不可能讓客人把兩個貨款合併一起付，危害我們的現金流。

▶ 語言陷阱 Language Traps:

1. We have already explained NCP costs and cash flow due to re-

ceiving defectives from LH Group.

我們已經解釋了因為收到LH集團的瑕疵品，而產生NCP成本跟現金流問題。

2. It seems we have got the same response from your reply. We will not continue the discussion in this mail.

但我們好像收到你們一樣的回覆，在這封信裡我們不再繼續談這個問題了。

▶ **技法字詞 Tricky Words and Phrases:**

cash flow 現金流

correction (n.) 更正

新手任務 Your Mission:

客戶不付款，我們就不再出貨，策略奏效，預計可收到部分貨款，但客戶仍然咬定我們貨品有瑕疵造成他的現金流問題，你要怎麼回信？

試寫Now You Try: 請試寫於下方

（試寫後才翻頁）

　　客戶怕我們不出貨，而願意付一批拖延的貨款。這時我們須先緩和，因為收錢是長時的，還是需要跟客人維持合作關係（除非你不跟這客人合作了；若只能走法律途徑，耗時耗力花費不貲，還不一定能收回貨款）。

　　把客人鎖定在談論付款的問題，先不要回答品質的問題。所有的文句都與付款條件與時間相關，先釐清彼此對於付款時間認知的差異點（須提及清單紀錄記載的正確時間，使我方證據充分），對方對於我方的付款時間認知不同，卻沒有提出更正或正面回答付款問題，讓我們飽受苦等壓力。結尾則提出將來雙方可討論如何溝通調整付款時間。

▶ **語言祕訣 Language Tips:**

1. **釐清關鍵點**

   The time of the payment term is **the key problem** in our discussion.

   我們的討論關鍵在於付款條件的時間點。

2. **說明我方關鍵點之計算**

   We think the calculation is based on B/L day, not NCP receiving date.

   我們認為計算的基礎是「提單日」，而非NCP收貨時間。

3. **提出歷史紀錄**

   It has been so in each of your statement records: T/T within 60 days after B/L day.

   每個清單紀錄一直都是如此：提單日60天內電匯。

4. 提出無更正

   Never have we received any correction from your side.

   我們從來沒有收過你們方面的任何更正。

5. 重申付款條件一致性

   We have never changed or become stricter on payment.

   我們從來沒有改變或緊縮付款條件。

6. 重申付款時間一致性

   We have always given you the same 60 days **as you actually requested.**

   我們一直都是給你們相同的60天，如同你們所要求的。

7. 指出對方的模糊手法

   In the nearly past two months, LH did **not get any correct, prompt, or straight answer** about the payment.

   在過去將近兩個月時間裡，關於付款問題，LH 完全沒有收到任何正確、及時或是直接的回答。

8. 要求同理心

   Can you imagine the nervousness and pressure LH faced?

   你們可以想像我們所面對的緊張與壓力嗎？

9. 建議關鍵點進一步溝通

   We can **have further negotiation on** "T/T WITHIN 60 days after B/L day" or NCP receiving date.

   我們可以就「提單日60天內付款」或「NCP收貨日」做進一步溝通。

key problem 關鍵問題

calculation (n.) 計算

request (v.) 要求

prompt (adj.) 及時的

straight (adj.) 直接的

nervousness (n.) 緊張

pressure (n.) 壓力

negotiation (n.) 溝通

● 信件範例 Sample Letter:

我方發信給客戶 Our Email to the Client

Dear Steve,

The time of the payment term is the key problem in our discussion. We think the calculation is based on B/L DAY, not NCP receiving date. In fact, it has been so in each of your statement records: T/T within 60 days after B/L day. Never have we received any correction from your side every time the statement being sent or when the payment status being checked. We have never changed or become stricter on payment; we have always given you the same 60 days as you actually requested.

In the nearly past two months, LH did not get any correct, prompt, or straight answer about the payment. Can you imagine the nervousness and pressure LH faced?

We can have further negotiation on "T/T WITHIN 60 days after

B/L day" or "NCP receiving date."

    Best regards,

    Clair

親愛的史蒂夫：

　　我們的討論關鍵在於付款條件的時間點，我們認為計算的基礎是「提單日」，而非NCP收貨時間。事實上，每個清單紀錄一直都是如此：提單日60天內電匯。每次我們寄出清單或確認付款狀況時，從來沒有收過你們方面的任何更正。我們從來沒有改變或緊縮付款條件，我們一直都是給你們相同的60天，如同你們所要求的。

　　在過去將近兩個月時間裡，關於付款問題，LH完全沒有收到任何正確、及時或是直接的回答，你們可以想像我們所面對的緊張與壓力嗎？

　　我們可以就「提單日60天內付款」或「NCP收貨日」做進一步溝通。

　　誠摯祝福，

　　克萊兒

客戶回信 Client's Reply

Dear Clair,

    Please notify NCP freight agents for PO#1576 shipment booking and get back to us the booking information as soon as possible.

    Please see attached bank confirmation for the wire transfer payment of PO#1563, $48,550 today.

    Best Regards,

    Steve

親愛的克萊兒：

請通知NCP船務預訂PO#1576出貨，然後盡快告知我們預訂資訊。

請看附件今天電匯PO#1563, $48,550的銀行確認。

誠摯祝福，

史蒂夫

★★★★★★★★★★★★★收款目標達成★★★★★★★★★★★★

攻防許多回合後終於收到匯款，落袋為安！

仍有待解問題要處理，並接續進行下一批出貨安排之回覆。

Round 9
第九回合

🔵 新手任務 Your Mission:
收到部分貨款了，下一批出貨之前，你該處理什麼？

🔵 試寫Now You Try: 請試寫於下方

（試寫後才翻頁）

教戰守則 Insider Tips

確定在收到一批貨的錢後，這封信要回答關於品質的關鍵問題。另一個重點是，要回覆已收到貨款，並要對方確認貨款到期時間已更改爲 T/T within 90 days after B/L day（提單日後90天內電匯），註明下批貨付款到期確實日期，防止下次貨款被拖延的問題。

品質問題的重點要釐清：

(1) 對方之不良品檢查認定。

(2) 對方所謂不良品的確實證據。

(3) 要表明若真有$35,000美金的品質不良問題，我們就要採取法律程序。

以上重點如果不表明，最後清算貨款時，客戶會以這$35,000當依據來扣款。提到法律問題，關乎雙方的互信基礎，當然要問對方有何想法，除非不得已，生意人將本求利，誰都不想走上那一步。

結尾要確認下一批出貨日期。

▶ 語言祕訣 Language Tips:

1. **確認付款條件**

   Please confirm the payment term. It is changed to be T/T within 90 days after B/L day from the next new order.

   請確認付款條件從下個新訂單開始，已經改爲「提單日後90天內電匯」。

2. **契約明載日期**

   The payment date will **be noted** in our contract.

   付款日會明載於我們的合約內。

3. **釐清品質問題**

Regarding the quality of products, **we have a few points to clarify**.

關於產品品質的問題，我們有些重點要釐清。

4. **強調信任**

We have never questioned your quality inspection because we have trusted your expertise.

本公司基於信任貴公司的專業，從未懷疑過貴公司對於不良品的認定方式。

5. **我方標準程序**

It surely has violated our company's standard procedure to handle defectives.

但這實在是違反了本公司處理不良品的標準程序。

6. **懷疑對方提出之數據**

Whenever we have so-called defectives, we have had only a few photos that you provided and have had no order number or craft number and any exact data.

每當我們收到貴公司提出有所謂不良品時，你們除了給我們幾張照片外，並沒有提供單號或箱號，以及任何確實數據。

7. **質疑對方要求之合理性**

You mentioned handling defectives has cost you $35,000. If it is true, **it is overly excessive than what we can endure**.

你上封信提到，你們處理不良品的費用已近$35,000美金。若屬實，這已經遠遠超出我們能承受的範圍。

8. **暗示法律作為**

   Please list details for us **to prepare for legal proceedings**, or perhaps you have other thoughts.

   請詳細列出過去的不良明細，以便本公司準備法律程序，或貴公司有其他想法。

9. **反問合作基礎**

   We have more than ten years of business relationship. **Is our mutual trust so weak**?

   我們合作超過十幾年，難道彼此的互信這麼薄弱嗎？

▶ 關鍵字詞 Key Words and Phrases:

question (v.) 質疑

expertise (n.) 專業

so-called defectives 所謂瑕疵品

violate (v.) 違反

overly excessive 太超過

legal proceedings 法律程序

mutual trust 互信

● 信件範例 Sample Letter:

🐴 我方發信給客戶 Our Email to the Client

Dear Steve,

About payment,

1. PO#1563, $48,550 is received today.

2. Please confirm the payment term. It is changed to be T/T

WITHIN 90 DAYS AFTER B/L DAY from the next new order. The payment date will be noted in our contract.

Regarding the quality of products, we have a few points to clarify.

1. We have never questioned your quality inspection because we have trusted your expertise. But it surely has violated our company's standard procedure to handle defectives.

2. Whenever we have so-called defectives, we have had only a few photos that you provided and have had no order number or craft number and any exact data.

3. You mentioned handling defectives has cost you $35,000. If it is true, it is overly excessive than what we can endure. Please list details for us to prepare for legal proceedings, or perhaps you have other thoughts.

4. We have more than ten years of business relationship. Is our mutual trust so weak?

About the shipment of PO#1576:

We are waiting for your forwarder's schedule confirmation.

Best regards,

Clair

親愛的史蒂夫：

關於付款：

1. PO#1563, $48,550已經收到。

2. 請確認付款條件從下個新訂單開始，已經改為「提單日後90天內電匯」。付款日會明載於我們的合約內。

關於產品品質的問題，我們有些重點要釐清。

1. 本公司基於信任貴公司的專業，從未懷疑過貴公司對於不良品的認定方式，但這實在是違反了本公司處理不良品的標準程序。

2. 每當我們收到貴公司提出有所謂不良品時，你們除了給我們幾張照片外，並沒有提供單號或箱號，以及任何確實數據。

3. 你上封信提到，你們處理不良品的費用已近$35,000美金。若屬實，這已經遠遠超出我們能承受的範圍。請詳細列出過去的不良明細，以便本公司準備法律程序，或貴公司有其他想法。

4. 我們合作超過十幾年，難道彼此的互信這麼薄弱嗎？

關於訂單PO#1576：

我們在等待你船務確認日期。

誠摯祝福，

克萊兒

🐴 客戶回信 Client's Reply

Dear Clair,

NCP and LH need further communication to bridge the gap of our different views on the payment terms and the costs we mentioned for fixing the defectives.

Our emails on Feb. 10, 2015 (attachment) show mutual understanding on payment terms clearly: 60 days after arrival. NCP has always emailed you to verify the actual arrival date when there are a few days of difference from your ETA date. If there is almost no difference, then we do not need to correct the date. We have been doing so with LH since 2008 and have never had any misunderstanding on payment terms. NCP has set the payment terms 60 days after arrival with other suppliers overseas. We would like to keep it the same with LH: 60 days after arrival of goods. In our emails, we gave you the actual arrival date in order for you to adjust the due date of payment. If you disagree with the 60 days after arrival payment terms, we can negotiate further.

The reason we brought up NCP costs for inspecting and fixing the defectives was to show LH that we have been working together to solve the problem. NCP has no intention to claim costs from LH because we appreciate your cooperation for fixing defects and allowing adjustable payment due dates. As mentioned earlier, we have had no interest in making claims against LH. Instead, what we wanted was to explain to you that we both sides understand the way we have been working together, and to give a clear idea about how NCP has worked, with all the expenses, to fix LH defectives. We think LH should understand the details better so we send you the reports showing what we have found on the goods. Surely when you have the details, your inspection process can spot and fix the defectives before shipment. NCP will be able to save lots of time and expenses for not having to fix LH defectives. We are certain that LH will be able to improve your inspection process, to find and fix the defectives before shipment.

One of our examples is attached to show what we have done to improve LH's products. NCP replaced the handle with quality job before shipping to our customer. We only took photos of different types of defects, instead of every single photo for each piece of all defectives. By doing so, we trust that LH will see the problem types and take necessary measures to fix them.

If making claims was our purpose, we would certainly have made clear and detailed records about every single defect type and every single piece of defective. However, NCP has not requested any compensation for the expenses. We only want to make it clear that you recognize our efforts behind and understand that we both sides have worked to fix defectives together. More important, we appreciate that LH has provided us with negotiable payment due dates.

It is our hope to move forward with LH.

Best regards,

Steve

親愛的克萊兒：

NCP與LH需要進一步的溝通，以拉近我們在付款條件及上次我們提到的修理瑕疵品成本上的差異。

我們在2015年2月10日的電子郵件裡（附件）清楚地顯示彼此了解付款條件是收到貨之後的60天。當與你們的預計抵達日期有幾天差異時，NCP一向電郵真正的到貨日給你們確認。如果日期接近的話，我們不需要去更正任何日期。我們從2008年至今一直這麼做，並且從沒有過任何付款條件的誤會。NCP與其他國外的供應商都訂了收貨後60天的付款條件，我們想要與LH保持同樣的付款條件：收貨後60天。在我們的電子郵件裡，我們給你們確實的收貨日期好讓你們調整付款到期日。如果你們不同意收貨後60天的付款條件，我們可以進一步溝通。

我們提出NCP在檢查及修理瑕疵品的成本是為了要讓LH知道我們一直彼此合作解決問題。NCP沒有意圖向LH提出理賠，因為我們感謝你們在修理瑕疵品以及允許我們調整付款到期日的合作。我們先前提到，我們沒有興趣向LH提出理賠。我們只想向你們解釋，我們彼

此了解我們一直以來的合作方式，以及給你們一個清楚的概念，有關NCP如何對LH的瑕疵品進行修理，即使因此而產生各種費用。我們認為LH應該更了解細節，所以我們寄報告給你們以顯示我們在貨物裡發現什麼。當然你們有細節時，你們可以在出貨前的檢查過程中發現及修理瑕疵品，NCP將可省去許多時間及費用，因為不需要修理LH的瑕疵品了。我們確實相信LH可以改善檢查過程，在出貨前發現及修理瑕疵品。

我們附上一個例子，顯示我們為了改善LH產品的作法。NCP在出貨給客戶前，更換了好品質的把手，再寄給客戶。我們只拍下不同種類的瑕疵，而未替所有瑕疵品的每一物件各拍一張。我們這樣做是因為我們相信LH會看到問題種類，並採取必要的辦法來修理它們。

假如我們意在提出理賠，我們一定已經做好關於每種瑕疵種類及每件瑕疵品清楚詳細的紀錄，但是我們沒有向你們要求任何費用的賠償，我們只要向你們表明你們認可我們背後的努力以及了解我們彼此一起修理瑕疵品。更重要的是，我們感激LH給我們彈性的付款到期日。

我們希望與LH一起前進。

誠摯祝福，

史蒂夫

 客戶來信：重點解讀 Getting the Hidden Messages

客戶的來信與我們的想法一樣，不會走法律途徑。但客戶一樣不斷重複提到檢查及修理我們的瑕疵品，使他們增加的成本，意在要我們退讓付款條件。文中提到他寄給我們確實收貨日期「好讓我們調整付款到期日」，意思是「他們認為我們已經了解」他們會拖延付款，但我們卻完全不知道。客戶自行假設，卻未向我方確認，也未得到我方同意，卻

要我們接受。

　　另外，客戶與其他供應商約定收貨後60天付款與我們的合約付款條件並無關聯，而他們自行比照拖延付款，事實上並沒有得到我們的同意，但他卻感激在先，先發制人。

▶ 語言陷阱 Language Traps:

1. Our emails on Feb. 10, 2015 (attachment) show mutual under-standing on payment terms clearly: 60 days after arrival.
   我們在2015年2月10日的電子郵件裡（附件）清楚地顯示彼此了解付款條件是收到貨之後的60天。

2. We have been doing so with LH since 2008 and have never had any misunderstanding on payment terms.
   我們從2008年至今一直這麼做，並且從沒有過任何付款條件的誤會。

3. NCP has set the payment terms 60 days after arrival with other suppliers overseas. We would like to keep it the same with LH: 60 days after arrival of goods.
   NCP與其他國外的供應商都訂了收貨後60天的付款條件，我們想要與LH保持同樣的付款條件：收貨後60天。

4. In our emails, we gave you the actual arrival date in order for you to adjust the due date of payment.
   在我們的電子郵件裡，我們給你們確實的收貨日期好讓你們調整付款到期日。

5. NCP has no intention to claim costs from LH because we appre-ciate your cooperation for fixing defects and allowing adjust-able payment due dates.
   NCP沒有意圖向LH提出理賠，因為我們感謝你們在修理瑕疵

品以及允許我們調整付款到期日的合作。

6. We only want to make it clear that you recognize our efforts behind and understand that we both sides have worked to fix defectives together.

我們只要向你們表明你們認可我們背後的努力以及了解我們彼此一起修理瑕疵品。

7. More important, we appreciate that LH has provided us with negotiable payment due dates.

更重要的是，我們感激LH給我們彈性的付款到期日。

▶ 技法字詞 Tricky Words and Phrases:

bridge the gap of our different views 拉近差異

verify (v.) 確認

ETA (estimated time of arrival) 預計到達日

misunderstanding (n.) 誤會

intention (n.) 意圖

claim (v./n.) 理賠

give a clear idea 使……清楚

replace (v.) 更換

recognize (v.) 認可

effort (n.) 努力

negotiable (adj.) 可協調的

Round 10
第十回合

● 新手任務 Your Mission:
收到PO#1563貨款了，接下來要處理什麼？

● 試寫Now You Try: 請試寫於下方

（試寫後才翻頁）

教戰守則 Insider Tips

這封信看出客人願意繼續跟我們合作，所以我們要保留回信的彈性及空間，不用急著表態及答覆客人。

這封信交代船務出貨事宜即可。

▶ 語言祕訣 Language Tips:

1. **提供日期資訊**

   Your forwarder has sent **the schedule for** PO#1576.
   你的船務寄來訂單PO#1576的日期。

2. **與……確認**

   Please confirm with your forwarder for arrangement on time.
   請與你的船務確認以準時安排。

● 信件範例 Sample Letter:

我方發信給客戶 Our Email to the Client

Dear Steve,

Your forwarder has sent the schedule for PO#1576:

Container loading on 9/15 and ETD on 9/20.

Please confirm with your forwarder for arrangement on time.

Best regards,

Clair

親愛的史蒂夫：

你的船務寄來訂單PO#1576的日期：

裝運日為9月15日，預計出航日9月20日。

請與你的船務確認以準時安排。

誠摯祝福，

克萊兒

▶ **關鍵字詞 Key Words and Phrases:**

forwarder (n.) 船務

schedule (n.) 日期

loading (n.) 裝貨

ETD (estimated time of departure) 預計出航日

arrangement (n.) 安排

★★★★★★★★★★★★★★★目標達成★★★★★★★★★★★★★★

先前已收到匯款，下一批出貨安排完成，雙方繼續生意往來，目標達成。

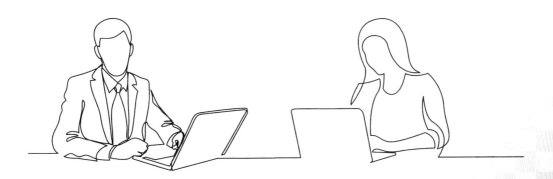

case 02 客戶因原物料降價要求降價
Client Requesting Price Reduction due to Lower Raw Material Cost

臺灣LH集團 vs 美國TOP AUTO集團

客戶與案例背景說明
Background of the Client and the Case

　　美國中部的客戶，進口商與零售商（實體及網路），六十多歲，大學畢業，早年在臺灣經商，對中國大陸也熟悉，是生意上的老江湖，雙方商業往來二十多年，但客戶卻慣性拖欠貨款，愈欠愈久，拖欠貨款目的愈來愈明顯。於2008年金融危機時，連續來信數封，每封皆要求降價，並提出鐵材降價，工資等數據。

　　我方如何因應？

Round 1
第一回合

客戶來信 Letter from the Client

Mr. Frank,

　　How are you? I hope you have enjoyed relaxing time in the Chinese New Year holidays.

　　For the new orders and the scheduling, we have discussed the costs and the shipment last month, but we have not gotten into discussing the American market. Overall, it has been rather flat. After Top

Auto developed innovative marketing methods, our sales have been growing, and we have been purchasing from LH Group for the orders.

Despite the good results, Top Auto has not been able to raise prices since 2008. In the current slack US economy, Top Auto does not have an opportunity to raise prices in the next season either.

As we will have a six-month new order schedule, we are asking LH Group a 5% price reduction from the date of the new order. The reason is obvious. Raw material has gone down since last year, and oil price is nearly 50% down. Your currency exchange gives you more edge. We are not intending to ask for reducing costs in all the aspects I mentioned. However, it is fair that your costs down reflect on our increase costs in shipment.

Another reason that has caused our need in price reduction is the costs of the shipment. For some complicated reasons, the total cost has gone up 55% instead of going down. Top Auto has no other solutions because we are unable to raise the price. We need help to take in this additional expense.

Melisa will be putting the order together. We are looking forward to working with you.

Henry Mathew

法蘭克先生：

你好嗎？希望你已經享受了輕鬆愉快的中國新年假期。

為了新訂單與計畫時程，我們上個月已經討論了成本跟運送，但我們還沒有討論到美國市場。整體來說，市場很平淡。在Top Auto發展出了創新的行銷方法之後，我們的銷售已經有所成長，而我們也持續在LH集團下訂單。

儘管有這些好結果，Top Auto自2008年起就無法提高售價。並且因為目前低迷的美國經濟，Top Auto在下一季也沒機會調高售價。

　　因為我們有六個月的新訂單計畫，我們要求LH集團自下個新訂單日起給我們5%的降價。原因很清楚，原料成本已經在去年就下降，油價也已經走跌50%，加上你們的貨幣匯率給你們優勢。我們並非要求我所提到的種種成本都要下降，但是你們的成本降價反映到對我們的運費成本上升才是公平的。

　　另外一個造成我們要求降價的原因是運費的成本，因為某些複雜的原因，總成本原本應該要下降，卻反而提高到55%。Top Auto因為無法漲價，沒有其他的解決辦法，我們需要你們幫忙吸收這個額外的成本。

　　瑪莉莎會把訂單弄好，我們期待與你們的合作。

　　亨利馬修

▶ 文化解析

　　稱謂之後理當使用姓氏，但稱謂後使用名字既顯示友善拉近距離又表示尊敬（Mr. Frank, Aunt Lucy, Uncle Bob），所以是一種常見的作法。背後的原因除了稱謂後用姓氏顯得較有距離之外，有些人的姓氏（尤其是民族熔爐國家）不僅該國的人不見得熟悉，對外國人而言更是摸不著頭緒，因此稱謂後使用名字是一種權宜的方式。

 客戶來信：重點解讀 Getting the Hidden Messages

　　客戶要求降價提出種種有利於自己的數據，長篇大論。最重要的原因是他向你採購，持續給你訂單，但市場卻景氣低迷，使他無法調漲產

品售價（過去跟將來皆然），所以要求你降價。其他原因還有原料價格下降、你的匯率貶值、他的運輸成本莫名上升。總而言之，他下訂單給你，也要你有難同當。

那麼他獲利有沒有分紅給你呢？他的數據對嗎？你要反駁他，跟他數據大戰嗎？他在布什麼局？引你進什麼陷阱呢？你要走進他所布的局嗎？如果客戶繼續來回死纏要求降價，你預計接下來如何攻防？

▶ **語言陷阱 Language Traps:**

1. After Top Auto developed innovative marketing methods, our sales have been growing, and we have been purchasing from LH Group for the orders.
   在Top Auto發展出了創新的行銷方法之後，我們的銷售已經有所成長，而我們也持續在LH集團下訂單。

2. Despite the good results, Top Auto has not been able to raise prices since 2008.
   儘管有這些好結果，Top Auto自2008年起就無法提高售價。

3. In the current slack US economy, Top Auto does not have an opportunity to raise prices in the next season either.
   目前低迷的美國經濟，Top Auto在下一季也沒機會調高售價。

4. As we will have a six-month new order schedule, we are asking LH Group a 5% price reduction from the date of the new order.
   因為我們有六個月的新訂單計畫，我們要求LH集團自下個新訂單日起給我們5%的降價。

5. The reason is obvious. Raw material has gone down since last year, and oil price is nearly 50% down.
   原因很清楚，原料成本已經在去年就下降，油價也已經走跌50%。

6. Your currency exchange gives you more edge.

   你們的貨幣匯率給你們優勢。

7. It is fair that your costs down reflect on our increase costs in shipment.

   你們的成本降價反映到對我們的運費成本上升才是公平的。

8. Another reason that has caused our need in price reduction is the costs of the shipment.

   另外一個造成我們要求降價的原因是運費的成本。

9. For some complicated reasons, the total cost has gone up 55% instead of going down.

   因為某些複雜的原因，總成本原本應該要下降，卻反而提高到55%。

10. Top Auto has no other solutions because we are unable to raise the price. We need help to take in this additional expense.

   Top Auto因為無法漲價，沒有其他的解決辦法，我們需要你們幫忙吸收這個額外的成本。

▶ 技法字詞 Tricky Words and Phrases:

flat (adj.) 平淡的

slack (adj.) 低迷的

raise (v.) 調漲

currency exchange 匯率

edge (n.) 優勢

reflect (v.) 反映

complicated (adj.) 複雜的

take in 吸收

 我方回信 Our Reply to the Client

Dear Henry,

　　We have to discuss with our material supplier and see if we have any conclusion.

　　Best,

　　Jessica

親愛的亨利：

　　我們會跟原物料的廠商討論看看是否有結論。

　　誠摯祝福，

　　潔西卡

Round 2
第二回合

客戶來信 Letter from the Client

Dear Frank,

　　Thank you for meeting me in China and bringing along the samples. It is our hope to add them to our line of products.

　　The attachment is a list of the raw materials we discussed. The prices have gone down as shown. Since the oil price has decreased, along with the reductions of the raw materilas, LH cost for Top Auto must have also become much lower. When the material costs increased, LH raised up the product price by 12%. Now the costs of the materials have gone down. LH must return Top Auto the price reduction to be fair.

Top Auto has to remain same pricing to our customers because of the slow economy, and the forecast does not see any uplifting in the coming year.

Mr. Frank, Top Auto has kept paying 12% price increase up to this day. Not only has Top Auto paid LH the huge price increase, but Top Auto has also increased orders of LH products. In addition, Top Auto has given LH the opportunity to be the supplier of various new items last year.

Now that the costs for the materials have all gone down, LH must work with Top Auto for price reduction.

Best regards,

Henry

親愛的法蘭克：

謝謝你到中國來與我會面，還帶來了樣品。我們希望可以把它們加到我們的產品項目。

附件是我們討論的原物料清單，價格（如顯示）已經降低了。因為油價已經降低，加上原物料降低，LH給Top Auto的成本一定也變得更低了。當原物料漲價時，LH產品漲價12%，現在原物料價格降低了，LH必須降價給Top Auto才公平。

因為經濟不景氣，Top Auto必須維持相同售價給顧客，而且預估接下來的一年景氣沒有一點上揚的跡象。

法蘭克先生，Top Auto到今天仍然持續付出12%的漲價，不僅付給LH巨大的漲價費用，Top Auto還增訂了很多產品。另外，Top Auto還給了LH機會成為去年許多新項目的供應商。

既然原物料成本已經下降，LH必須配合Top Auto降價。

誠摯祝福，

亨利

 客戶來信：重點解讀 Getting the Hidden Messages

客戶開啓戰場，來信要求降價，客人繼續來第二封信催促降價，長篇大論，所有的重點只有一個：要求降價。客人像海浪一波波，列出他認爲我們要降價的原因（最大原因是：原物料及油價下降，並且我們在原物料上漲時曾經漲過價）。

客戶丟出一個個非降價不可的理由，並且在信中再次稱呼主管名字必須降價，讀起來令人壓迫感十足。但從另一方面來看，雖然降價馬上就面臨侵蝕利潤的問題，但客戶會寫長信給我們，也是看重我們，至少把我們當作優先採購的第一順序。

▶ **語言陷阱 Language Traps:**

1. Since the oil price has decreased, along with the reductions of the raw matierlas, LH cost for Top Auto must have also become much lower.

   因爲油價已經降低，加上原物料降低，LH給Top Auto的成本一定也變得更低了。

2. When the material costs increased, LH raised up the product price by 12%.

   當原物料漲價時，LH產品漲價12%。

3. Now the costs of the materials have gone down. LH must return Top Auto the price reduction to be fair.

   現在原物料價格降低了，LH必須降價給Top Auto才公平。

4. Top Auto has to remain same pricing to our customers because of the slow economy.

因為經濟不景氣，Top Auto必須維持相同售價給顧客。

5. The forecast does not see any uplifting in the coming year.

預估接下來的一年景氣沒有一點上揚的跡象。

6. Not only has Top Auto paid LH the huge price increase, but Top Auto has also increased orders of LH products.

Top Auto不僅付給LH巨大的漲價費用，Top Auto還增訂了很多產品。

7. In addition, Top Auto has given LH the opportunity to be the supplier of various new items last year.

另外，Top Auto還給了LH機會成為去年許多新項目的供應商。

8. Now that the costs for the materials have all gone down, LH must work with Top Auto for price reduction.

既然原物料成本已經下降，LH必須配合Top Auto降價。

▶ 技法字詞 Tricky Words and Phrases:

forecast (n.) 預估

uplifting (n.) 上揚

● 新手任務 Your Mission:

如何四兩撥千斤回答降價問題？

● 試寫Now You Try: 請試寫於下方

（試寫後才翻頁）

教戰守則 Insider Tips

面對降價要求，不需要急著回。接受客戶要求容易，卻可能害公司虧本做白工；直接回答「No」也會直接惹惱客戶。多數利潤微薄的公司，必須懂得如何婉拒客戶的要求，或僅作微小的退讓。

第一句開宗明義說明無法降價，解釋原因，歸納結論：無法降價，結尾感謝及期待繼續合作。記住第一封回覆時不提數據，提供數據可能反而進入數據大戰，或進一步被客戶瓦解而洞悉成本。總之，第一回合回覆先簡短，寫一段就好，不要寫長，愈長愈容易被挑到問題，下封再看他如何出招。

▶ **語言祕訣 Language Tips:**

1. **點出公司經營原則**

   It has always been our company policy to offer our customers the best services and the most competitive prices.

   給客人最好的服務及最具有競爭力的價格，一直都是本公司的原則。

2. **告知售價計算結果**

   After recalculating all costs again for your order, **we confirm that** the price remains unchanged.

   經過本公司的仔細計算，我們確定售價維持不變。

3. **解釋原因一**

   Although the iron price has gone down a little lately, the labor costs in production, in-land delivery, and international shipment **have rocketed in recent years**.

   雖然鐵材近來有下降一些，但生產製造的人工成本，內陸運

輸及國際運輸成本近年來一飛沖天。

4. **解釋原因二**

   In addition, **the increases of** the taxes and labor insurances have been imposed upon us.
   此外，各種稅金及勞工保險的增加也被強加進我們的成本。

5. **要求同理心（面臨持續變動的處境）**

   With all kinds of costs going up drastically, **you can see what business environment we are facing** now to meet China's ever-increasing demands.
   面對所有劇烈的成本上升，您可以理解我們爲了配合中國不斷增加的要求，目前正面臨何種商業處境。

6. **感謝支持**

   We are obliged to your kind support over the years **and look forward to** your continuing business in the future.
   我們不會忘記您多年來的支持，期待您將來的持續關照。

▶ **關鍵字詞** Key Words and Phrases:

competitive (adj.) 競爭力的

recalculate (v.) 重新計算

labor costs in production 生產的人工成本

in-land delivery 內陸運輸

international shipment 國際運輸

rocket (v.) 急速升高

labor insurance 勞工保險

impose (v.) 強加

ever-increasing (adj.) 不斷增加的

drastically (adv.) 劇烈地

demand (n.) 需求

be obliged 心懷感激的

信件範例 Sample Letter:

我方發信給客戶 Our Email to the Client

Dear Mr. Henry,

It has always been our company policy to offer our customers the best services and the most competitive prices. After recalculating all costs again for your order, we confirm that the price remains unchanged. Although the iron price has gone down a little lately, the labor costs in production, in-land delivery, and international shipment have rocketed in recent years. In addition, the increases of the taxes and labor insurances have been imposed upon us. With all kinds of costs going up drastically, you can see what business environment we are facing now to meet China's ever-increasing demands. We are obliged to your kind support over the years and look forward to your continuing business in the future.

Most sincerely yours,

Frank

親愛的亨利先生：

給客人最好的服務及最具有競爭力的價格，一直都是本公司的原則。因此，經過本公司的仔細計算，我們確定售價維持不變。雖然鐵材近來有下降一些，但生產製造的人工成本、內陸運輸及國際運輸成

本近年來一飛沖天，此外，各種稅金及勞工保險的增加也被強加進我們的成本。面對所有成本劇烈地上升，您可以理解我們為了配合中國不斷增加的要求，目前正面臨何種商業處境。我們公司不會忘記您多年來的支持，期待您將來的持續關照。

極誠摯地，
法蘭克

▶ 進入第三回合之前的心理準備與策略

客戶會寫這麼長的信，提出一堆數據就表示後續可能會死纏爛打，需要來往攻防幾回才能搞定。客戶想繼續爭取降價，就會提出只利於他自己的數據，或引用競爭對手低價來殺價。當然為了雙方長久利益，衡量情形，做出些微的讓步並非不可行，但幅度應當僅限於些微，這部分預計可能在往返數回合後發生。

Round 3
第三回合

 客戶來信 Client's Letter

---

Mr. Frank,

The cost of a 20 foot container has increased in the last six months, from $3,500 to $5,300. Top Auto is unable to pass the freight increase to our customers. Since 2008, we have not had any opportunity to raise prices.

Although some of your costs have gone up, but raw material, oil, and your currency have all gone down. We have done what you asked to expand business with you and your business has erupted. With the

---

extended order, LH can absorb the 5% reduction in the next season to help Top Auto's increased costs.

Thank you for understanding our situation.

Best regards,

Henry Mathew

法蘭克先生：

20呎的貨櫃成本過去六個月已經從$3,500漲到$5,300。Top Auto沒有辦法轉嫁運費給我們的顧客。自2008年起我們就沒有機會漲價。

雖然你的一些成本上升，但原物料、油價跟你的貨幣已經下降，我們按照你所要求的擴充生意，你的事業已爆炸成長。LH有能力在下一季裡吸收5%的降價來幫助Top Auto所增加的成本。

謝謝你體諒我們的情況。

誠摯祝福，

亨利馬修

 客戶來信：重點解讀 Getting the Hidden Messages

這次客戶來信繼續算他的成本給你聽，重複上次信件內容說市況差，他無法調漲，無法將成本轉嫁給顧客，然後計算你的成本大降，重點是你還因為他給的訂單大賺一筆，所以你應該要體諒他，至少要給他5%的降價空間。

▶ 語言陷阱 Language Traps:

1. The cost of a 20 foot container has increased in the last six months, from $3,500 to $5,300.

20呎的貨櫃成本過去六個月已經從$3,500漲到$5,300。

2. Top Auto is unable to pass the freight increase to our customers. Since 2008, we have not had any opportunity to raise prices.

Top Auto沒有辦法轉嫁運費給我們的顧客。自2008年起我們就沒有機會漲價。

3. Although some of your costs have gone up, but raw material, oil, and your currency have all gone down.

雖然你的一些成本上升，但原物料、油價跟你的貨幣已經下降。

4. We have done what you asked to expand business with you and your business has erupted.

我們按照你所要求的擴充生意，你的事業已爆炸成長。

5. With the extended order, LH can absorb the 5% reduction in the next season to help Top Auto's increased costs.

LH有能力在下一季裡吸收5%的降價來幫助Top Auto所增加的成本。

6. Thank you for understanding our situation.

謝謝你體諒我們的情況。

▶ 技法字詞 Tricky Words and Phrases:

raw material 原物料

expand (v.) 擴充

erupt (v.) 爆炸

extend (v.) 延伸

absorb (v.) 吸收

reduction (n.) 減少

situation (n.) 情況

　　客人不會想知道或同情你的處境，認為他下訂給你生意，你要面對他的處境，有求必應，趕快解決他的問題。連續來兩封長信，彼此耐性快磨光，接下來你該怎麼回答？

● 試寫Now You Try: 請試寫於下方

（試寫後才翻頁）

教戰守則 Insider Tips

正如預料，客戶持續丟來數據哀號他的成本上升，緊咬你成本下降部分，要求你降價。可考慮在這封信作出非常些微的讓步，就此打住，一來顯示你成本仍然非常高昂，二來顯示你有聽進去，已給予誠意的回應。

▶ 語言祕訣 Language Tips:

1. 表示同理心

   We fully understand your situation, and this is also the same here.

   我們完全理解你的情形，因為這裡的情形是一樣的。

2. 重申價格

   After calculating the cost, 25256 price at USD20.47/pc (FOB / Shanghai) **is really the bottom** on our side and can be active for the new orders.

   計算成本後，25256的價格，每件定價美金20.47（上海離岸價）已經是我們的底價，並且可開始接受新訂單。

3. 表達期望

   (We) sincerely hope to receive your acceptance by return.

   誠摯希望收到您的回覆同意。

▶ 關鍵字詞 Key Words and Phrases:

calculate (v.) 計算

bottom (n.) 底部

active (adj.) 主動的，有效的

acceptance (n.) 接受

信件範例 Sample Letter:

我方發信給客戶 Our Email to the Client

Dear Henry,

We fully understand your situation, and this is also the same here.

After calculating the cost, 25256 price at USD20.47/pc (FOB Shanghai) is really the bottom on our side and can be active for the new orders.

Sincerely hope to receive your acceptance by return.

Frank

親愛的亨利：

我們完全理解你的情形，因為這裡的情形是一樣的。

計算成本後，25256的價格，每件定價美金20.47（上海離岸價）已經是我們的底價，並且可開始接受新訂單。

誠摯希望收到您的回覆同意。

法蘭克

Round 4
第四回合

客戶來信 Client's Letter

Mr. Frank,

Your discount must be a mistake. $0.25 reduction does not help Top Auto for the reasons below.

1. LH has increased 12% two years ago.

2. The costs have gone down.

3. DD Beat gives major distributors 20% below our price. How do you explain that you provide them $18 per piece?

Mr. Frank, we have kept asking for your help, but you do nothing while Top Auto has continuously given you great sales. For our new orders, it is hard for us to justify the purchases for the unequal situation you have made for our company.

It is only fair for you to consider leveling the playing field between DD Beat and Top Auto. There is no reason why DD Beat gets a favorable price while Top Auto does not. Something must be done!

Henry

法蘭克先生：

　　你的折扣一定是算錯了，$0.25根本沒辦法幫助Top Auto，原因如下：

1. LH 兩年前曾經漲價12%。

2. 成本已經降價。

3. DD Beat給大經銷商比我們還低20%的價格，你如何解釋你提供他們每件$18的價格？

　　法蘭克先生，我們一直要求你的幫忙，但當Top Auto持續給你大訂單時，你什麼也沒做。我們很難認為你這樣對我們公司不公平的情況，對我們的新訂單是正當的。

　　只有你考慮給DD Beat跟我們同樣的競爭環境才公平。沒有任何理由DD Beat得到優惠的價格，而Top Auto卻沒有。你必須採取行動！

　　亨利

客戶來信：重點解讀 Getting the Hidden Messages

客戶在信件內文裡叫名字，無非就是要你注意到他的火大。客戶舉出你應當降價的三大理由及拿別家的價錢（產品不同）要求你降價，並且很不客氣地說他公司給你賺大錢，但你卻對他們的要求視若無睹，要你採取行動，快快答應降價。

▶ 語言陷阱 Language Traps:

1. Your discount must be a mistake.
   你的折扣一定是算錯了。

2. LH has increased 12% two years ago.
   LH 兩年前曾經漲價12%。

3. The costs have gone down.
   成本已經降價。

4. DD Beat gives major distributors 20% below our price. How do you explain that you provide them $18 per piece?
   DD Beat給大經銷商比我們還低20%的價格，你如何解釋你提供他們每件$18的價格？

5. We have kept asking for your help, but you do nothing while Top Auto has continuously given you great sales.
   我們一直要求你的幫助，但當Top Auto持續給你大訂單時，你什麼也沒做。

6. For our new orders, it is hard for us to justify the purchases for the unequal situation you have made for our company.
   我們很難認為你這樣對我們公司不公平的情況，對我們的新訂單是正當的。

7. It is only fair for you to consider leveling the playing field between DD Beat and Top Auto.

只有你考慮給DD Beat跟我們同樣的競爭環境才公平。

8. There is no reason why DD Beat gets a favorable price while Top Auto does not.

沒有任何理由DD Beat得到優惠的價格，而Top Auto卻沒有。

9. Something must be done!

你必須採取行動！

▶ 技法字詞 Tricky Words and Phrases:

increase (v.) 上漲，增加

major distributor 主要經銷商

justify (v.) 證明為正當的

unequal (adj.) 不平等的

level (v.) 使平等

playing field 戰場，球場

favorable (adj.) 有利的

● 新手任務 Your Mission:

在商言商，我們當然會因為不同客戶，購買不同產品，使用不同交易條件（材質、包裝、運輸……），而有不同定價。客戶或許也知道舉他人的例子未必恰當，但無論如何他都要拿來相提並論，當談判籌碼。至此階段客人已耐性全無，語氣飽受委屈，直接要你降價5%解決問題。你要如何回答？

（試寫後才翻頁）

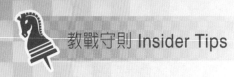
我們的目的是不傷和氣，還要他把舊款付了，他也要顧及自己面子跟誠信，自己找臺階下，如此他清償舊債，而我們新的訂單也到手，還要客人遵守下次付款準時。

以感謝開場，感謝結尾，內容重點要解釋客戶產品條件不同，保證他有最好品質的產品，公司成本不斷精簡控制，如此的價格已是最低價，客戶必須了解能獲得降價的條件是準時付款，我們此時可略降__%，已是最大降幅。

▶ 語言祕訣 Language Tips:

1. **感謝支持**

   We are thankful for your continuing support over the years.

   感謝你的來信，也很感謝你多年來，對本公司持續的支持。

2. **釐清客戶所指售價高並非事實**

   Your mentioning in the letter about DD Beat's buying or selling price is **neither correct nor valid in our understanding**.

   對於你在信中所提到，關於DD Beat的買價或賣價，就我們的了解，並不正確也非有效。

3. **指出出貨包裝要求造成價格差異**

   We guarantee that both prices are on the same quoting basis but **different in** packaging for shipment.

   我們能給你保證的是，你們兩家的價格在相同的基準上，但是你們出貨的包裝要求是不一樣的。

4. 表示願意小幅讓步

It is impossible for us to lower 5% to meet your request soon. **However, we can offer** 1.5% discount maximum at this point of time.

本公司短期內無法配合你要我們降價5%的請求，但我們願意提供在這時間點最大1.5%降幅的折扣。

5. 解釋已自行撙節成本

To maintain the best quality and the best price, we have always been cutting costs and expenses over the years to **strive for top efficiency**.

過去這些年，爲了維持最好的價格及產品的品質，我們每年都會自行撙節成本，削減開支。

6. 提醒「準時付款」爲記帳客戶之根本

We would like to remind you that making payments according to the contract schedule is **the basis of** our client credibility for an open account.

我們也要提醒您，按照合約時間付款是我們記帳客戶信用的基準。

7. 表示經濟局勢非我方能控制

We hope that you will understand that the situation and the factors are **beyond our control**.

我們希望您能了解現今的情況跟因素非我們所能控制。

8. 感謝與承諾最好之品質價格

Despite our inability to help this time, **we are positive that** we will continue our business relationship because we only offer you our best quality products and the best pricing!

雖然我們此時無法幫忙，我們有信心將來與您持續合作，因為我們只提供您最好品質的產品與最好的價格！

▶ 關鍵字詞 Key Words and Phrases:

valid (adj.) 有效的

guarantee (v.) 保證

packaging (n.) 包裝

meet your request 符合你的要求

discount maximum 最大折扣

strive (v.) 努力

remind (v.) 提醒

credibility (n.) 信用

信件範例 Sample Letter:

我方發信給客戶 Our Email to the Client

Dear Henry,

We are thankful for your continuing support over the years.

Your mentioning in the letter about DD Beat's buying or selling price is neither correct nor valid in our understanding. We guarantee that both prices are on the same quoting basis but different in packaging for shipment.

Regarding price, it is impossible for us to lower 5% to meet your request soon. However, we can offer 1.5% discount maximum at this point of time. To maintain the best quality and the best price, we have always been cutting costs and expenses over the years to strive for top efficiency. By the way, we would like to remind you that making payments according to the contract schedule is the basis of our client credibility for an open account.

We hope that you will understand that the situation and the factors are beyond our control. Despite our inability to help this time, we are positive that we will continue our business relationship because we only offer you our best quality products and the best pricing!

Sincerely,

Frank

親愛的亨利：

感謝你的來信，也很感謝你多年來，對本公司持續的支持。

對於你在信中所提到，關於DD Beat的買價或賣價，就我們的了解，並不正確也非有效。我們能給你保證的是，你們兩家的價格在相同的基準上，但是你們出貨的包裝要求是不一樣的。

有關價格方面，本公司短期內無法配合你要我們降價5%的請求，但我們願意提供在這時間點最大1.5%降幅的折扣。過去這些年，為了維持最好的價格及產品的品質，我們每年都會自行撙節成本，削減開支。我們也要提醒您，按照合約時間付款是我們記帳客戶信用的基準。

我們希望您能了解現今的情況跟因素非我們所能控制，雖然我們此時無法幫忙，我們有信心將來與您持續合作，因為我們只提供您最好品質的產品與最好的價格！

誠摯祝福，

法蘭克

客戶回信 Client's Reply

Frank,

Top Auto would order 250 tool kits if you agree to pay for the increased freight. Our margins are too low to pay for the extra shipping expenses. LH should keep your promise in May to ship our first container on time. We agree to accept the partial payment if you pay for the 250 tool kits interim shipment and the extra shipment charges.

Henry

法蘭克：

如果你同意付運費，Top Auto將訂購250個工具箱，我們的利潤低到無法支付額外的運輸費用。LH應該遵守五月時的承諾，準時將第一批貨櫃出貨。如果你支付250個工具箱過渡期的運費及額外運輸費用，我們同意接受部分付款。

亨利

 客戶來信：重點解讀 Getting the Hidden Messages

客戶舊款未清，新單砍價未果，便以少量的新訂單（250個工具箱）誤導我們接單，依他的布局進行下去。因數量並未達到最少訂購量（MOQ），所以我們必須要求增加數量符合我們的MOQ，並還清任何欠款，或購買其他貨品，才能答應降價。注意客戶並不明說他「同意接受部分付款」指的是什麼，用意在於誘使我們同意接受此訂單，付款方

面還可能另有玄機。

　若我們不要此訂單，是不是有更多的空間？客人要求第一批貨櫃出貨（因為客人沒付款，所以我們停止出貨），如果這250個工具箱運輸時間不一樣，不同的櫃子如何出貨，這250個工具箱的貨款或全部貨款最後收款的時間，是否反而被拖延？

▶ 語言陷阱 Language Traps:

1. Top Auto would order 250 tool kits if you agree to pay for the increased freight.
   如果你同意付運費，Top Auto將訂購250個工具箱。

2. LH should keep your promise in May to ship our first container on time.
   LH應該遵守五月時的承諾，準時將第一批貨櫃出貨。

3. We agree to accept the partial payment if you pay for the 250 tool kits interim shipment and the extra shipment charges.
   如果你支付250個工具箱過渡期的運費及額外運輸費用，我們同意接受部分付款。

▶ 技法字詞 Tricky Words and Phrases:

keep your promise (keep your word, honor your commitment)
守信
eat your word 食言
margin (n.) 利潤
promise (n.) 承諾
partial payment 部分付款
interim (adj.) 過渡的
charge (n.) 費用

客人並未回答是否接受1.5%的降價,但想下另一個訂單要你付運費,你該如何回信?這等同變相降價,可能幅度更甚,並且跟前面所提是不同產品,等於是新闢不同產品的攻防戰,移花接木,你要怎麼接招呢?

● 試寫Now You Try: 請試寫於下方

（試寫後才翻頁）

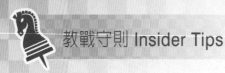

教戰守則 Insider Tips

　　回覆降價要求的不變定律是強調價格的關鍵在於品質。一旦開起降價之門，就開啟惡性循環，除非雙方都只想向下沉淪，做次級品或劣質產品。如果你的產品品質經得起考驗，客戶無法不向你購買就一定會回頭。只管降價不問品質的客人不是長期合作的對象，降價可能造成客戶不知珍惜還看不起產品，覺得可以一直降價。堅守立場，反而可以贏得尊敬。

　　另可考慮引用以前交易及沒有理賠紀錄還提供永久保固，證明自己沒有再降價空間，並且不要進入對方數據大戰的圈套。溝通結束時要再次強調品質與合理價格才能維持雙方合作的長久關係。

▶ 語言祕訣 Language Tips:

1. **表示出價過低**

   Your proposed price is **far below** our quote.
   您的出價遠低於我們的報價。

2. **告知報價已屬優惠**

   We have provided you **favorable pricing**!
   我們提供您的報價已屬優惠！

3. **要求提供測試標準（或其他要求）分析估價**

   If you offer testing standards or other requirements for our reference, we can take all factors into consideration and **analyze pricing again**.
   貴公司是否可以先提供測試的標準，或其他的要求給本公司參考，以便我們做價格的分析及調整。

4. 刺激對方追求優良產品

But in the long run, **we do not think second class quality products are what we both want**.

但長期而言，我們並不認爲我們雙方想追求的是次級品。

▶ 關鍵字詞 Key Words and Phrases:

proposed price 出價

quote (n.) 報價

testing standards 檢驗標準

take all factors into consideration 納入所有因素考量

analyze pricing 分析價格

in the long run 長期

Dear Henry,

Your proposed price is far below our quote. As you surely know the price is determined by quality and quantity in each order. We have provided you favorable pricing! If you offer testing standards or other requirements for our reference, we can take all factors into consideration and analyze pricing again. But in the long run, we do not think second class quality products are what we both want.

Regards,

Frank

親愛的亨利：

您的出價遠低於我們的報價。您一定了解每張訂單的定價都取決於品質與數量，我們提供您的報價已屬優惠！貴公司是否可以先提供測試的標準，或其他的要求給本公司參考，以便我們做價格的分析及調整，但長期而言，我們並不認為我們雙方想追求的是次級品。

誠摯祝福，

法蘭克

★★★★★★★★★★★★★目標達成★★★★★★★★★★★★★★

經過5回合的攻防，我方守住該客戶該產品些微的1.5%降價。

case **03**

客戶因匯率變動要求降價
Client Requesting Price Reduction due to Exchange Rate Changes

---

臺灣LH集團 vs 美國LEGEND DEAL集團

客戶與案例背景說明
Background of the Client and the Case

　　無論什麼客戶，總會趁著匯率變動時，要來殺價，客戶的陳述是事實。因為市場環境的變化，美金升值，出口國貨幣（新臺幣或人民幣）相對貶值，客人趁此時機要求降價，但相對的也可猜出客戶要下單了。

Round 1
第一回合

客戶來信 Client's Letter

Dear Frank,

　　China's exchange rate to USD has been devalued from RMB 6.05: $1 to RMB 6.25: $1 in the past two weeks and seems to become stable now. For our long business history and our future business, we should adjust price according to the changes. Please let us know what you think.

　　Best,

　　Ryne

親愛的法蘭克：

　　中國的人民幣兌美元的匯率已經在過去的兩週內從人民幣6.05元兌1美元貶值到人民幣6.25元兌1美元，並且現在似乎穩定下來了。為了我們的長期商務歷史與將來合作，我們應當按照這些改變調整價錢，請告訴我你的想法。

　　誠摯祝福，

　　萊恩

● 新手任務 Your Mission:

　　我方匯率貶值事實上對工廠出口有利，在過去的商業模式中，我方曾降價給其他客戶，但若此時我方不想降價，該如何回信呢？

● 試寫Now You Try: 請試寫於下方

（試寫後才翻頁）

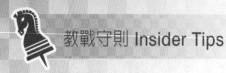
教戰守則 Insider Tips

　　我們要馬上想到客戶訂單的貨物數量跟貨物種類與金額有多少？貨物要運到哪裡？注意客戶可能隨便先給數量，我方也必須考慮季節變化，判斷客人所言數量真假。

　　我們有兩種方式來回應客戶的降價要求：

1. 說明國際局勢與我方的困難。

    (1) 美國總統大選，川普聲勢上漲，增添貿易變數。

    (2) 韓國韓進貨輪公司破產，造成運輸費用上漲。

    (3) 中國第三季開始，工資平均上漲6.5%，社會保險也跟著調高。

    (4) 中國人又在搶買房子，建築商又在搶地搶建房屋，間接造成鋼鐵需求上漲。

2. 利用業務本身為勞方的關係，攻敵需先攻心，激起客戶（同屬勞方）的同理心，使用苦肉計。當然還要提醒客戶「加量訂購」也是可能降價的方法之一。

▶ 語言祕訣 Language Tips:

1. 指出價格不利，激發同理心

You have **given my boss a good reason** not to raise our salary this year.

你提醒我的老闆今年不給我們加薪的好理由。

2. 價格協議反問

He is asking if you'll agree to accept price increase at the same percentage **when RMB bounces back**.

他問貴公司是否同意當人民幣升值時，調回相同的百分比？

3. 期望增加採購量

We hope that you'll **increase purchase** this year.
我們期望貴公司今年可以增加採購量。

▶ 關鍵字詞 Key Words and Phrases:

raise salary 加薪
price increase 漲價
bounce back 彈回
increase purchase 加購

● 信件範例 Sample Letter:

♞ 我方發信給客戶 Our Email to the Client

Dear Ryne,

　　You have given my boss a good reason not to raise our salary this year after I mentioned reducing price. He is asking if you'll agree to accept price increase at the same percentage when RMB bounces back, and we hope that you'll increase purchase this year.

　　Thank you and have a nice weekend!

　　James

親愛的萊恩：

　　你提醒我的老闆今年不給我們加薪的好理由。我向我老闆報告後，他問貴公司是否同意當人民幣升值時，調回相同的百分比？我們期望貴公司今年可以增加採購量。

　　謝謝，並祝有個美好的週末！

　　詹姆士

 客戶回信 Client's Reply

Dear James,

As a buyer, you know I have to ask all kinds of questions. I have talked to our customers and they can accept the current price. I hope you get what you work for.

Ryne

親愛的詹姆士：

身為採購者，你知道我必須要問各種問題，我已經跟客戶談過，他們可以接受現在的價格，我希望你可以得到你的工作所得。

萊恩

 客戶來信：重點解讀 Getting the Hidden Messages

客戶顯然用同樣的信給其他供應商，而其他供應商就降價給客戶，既然他已經在其他地方得到降價，我方未降價就不成問題了，顯見我方的策略奏效。

🗨 新手任務 Your Mission:

你必須回覆客戶的善意（不讓客戶繼續要求降價），並且你還要讓他快下訂。

試寫Now You Try: 請試寫於下方

（試寫後才翻頁）

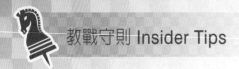

　除感謝客人的諒解外，也要告訴客人，本公司不是鐵板一塊不能講價的，若不這麼說，怕客戶跑去跟其他的工廠買，不跟你交易了。

▶ **語言祕訣 Language Tips:**

1. **感謝理解**

Thank you for your understanding so we can continue our business relationship.

謝謝你的理解，讓我們的合作能夠持續。

2. **指出目前價格有利雙贏**

With the current pricing, we can reassure the best quality of our products. It is what **we both pursue, a win-win solution** for our companies.

以目前的價格，我們可以再次保證產品的良好品質。我們所追求的是我們彼此的公司能夠雙贏的方案。

3. **告知採購計畫，有利價格調整**

If you have any **new orders or plans** for this year, please let me know now. I may have an opportunity to try to adjust the price.

如果你今年有任何新的訂單或計畫，請現在告訴我，我會去爭取價格做適當的調整。

▶ **關鍵字詞 Key Words and Phrases:**

reassure (v.) 再次保證

win-win solution 雙贏方案

new orders or plans 新訂單或計畫

adjust the price 調整價格

我方發信給客戶 Our Email to the Client

Dear Ryne,

Thank you for your understanding so we can continue our business relationship. Of course, with the current pricing, we can reassure the best quality of our products. It is what we both pursue, a win-win solution for our companies. If you have any new orders or plans for this year, please let me know now. I may have an opportunity to try to adjust the price.

James

親愛的萊恩：

謝謝你的理解，讓我們的合作能夠持續，當然以目前的價格，我們可以再次保證產品的良好品質。我們所追求的是我們彼此的公司能夠雙贏的方案。如果你今年有任何新的訂單或計畫，請現在告訴我，我會去爭取價格做適當的調整，謝謝！

詹姆士

客人來信 Client's Reply

Hi, James,

Got it. Thank you.

Ryne

嗨，詹姆士：

收到了，謝謝。

萊恩

★★★★★★★★★★★★★★目標達成★★★★★★★★★★★★★★

經過三回合攻防，客人來信表示了解，我方守住未因匯率變動而降價，目標達成！

註：如果一開始採取解釋國際情勢及我方苦處，客人可能會用國際情勢或客戶的市場狀況處理回信，引起雙方許多回合的辯論，來回信件可能造成語意誤會，結果不是我方敗陣而被迫降價，就是客人即使接受我方不降價，也可能心裡不愉快。

客戶以品質為由在新單殺價索賠
Client Complaining Quality for Price Reduction and Product Replacement

臺灣LH集團 vs 新加坡ENGINE KING集團

客戶與案例背景說明
Background of the Client and the Case

　　美籍新加坡華人二代進出口商兄妹檔，哥哥為總經理約四十多歲，在美國取得大學及碩士商學位，妹妹取得美國高中及大學商學位，擔任公司採購，此公司為當地大盤商，向我方進貨提供馬來西亞數十家年長者經營的五金雜貨店（俗稱papa mama shop）。

　　該公司每週派員去幫忙店家結帳補貨，所以年長者可就業，但只會簡單記帳，不會修理，無法搬貨，也不太會換進貨商，甚至不會去銀行存錢（由銀行保全收帳），全由大盤商一手包。換句話說，這類老舊五金店等於是大盤商的綿密銷售點兼倉庫，也是網路銷售到店取貨的一種方式。

　　與此兄妹檔客戶過去交易的經驗顯示，客戶做幾筆生意後，總是抱怨品質有問題，下筆新訂單前就試圖用品質不良的理由來殺價。若殺價不成，就會要求賠償前幾筆交易的不良品。

　　這次客戶剛收到一批50臺的貨後，不久後來信宣稱其中一項產品有2臺有問題，顯然客戶想故技重施，對下次新訂貨時保留殺價或扣款的空間。這位客人很聰明的叫他們自己的工程師撥電話給我方業務說明產品問題所在，而且於電話中語意不詳要求賠償數量。經過電話數次溝通後，我方仍須面對面飛去新加坡會議解決。

會議主談人雙方為其妹妹及其工程師與我方兩位人員，但因我方未做會議紀錄，結果啞巴吃黃蓮。客人來信要求處理不良品，來信所描述的內容，與事實有些出入，但這個錯誤在於我方跟客戶開完會後（或講完電話後），沒有馬上把會議紀錄給客戶確認。

Round 1
第一回合

客戶來信 Client's Reply

Dear Reese,

We need your conclusion on sending us 50 pieces of CPCs as replacement. It's been over four months since we pointed out this problem to you at the office in person. We have already talked on the phone and on your visit about this matter. As you know, our customers are waiting for the solution to solve the problem for a long time. We hope that you understand our difficult situation and kindly assist us as soon as possible to provide the 50 pieces of CPCs to close the case.

We look forward to your prompt reply. Thank you.

Best regards,

Andrew

親愛的瑞絲：

我們需要你為替換50個CPCs做個結論，自從我們在辦公室親自向你指出這個問題到現在已經四個多月了，我們已經在電話中以及你來訪的時候討論過這件事，你知道我們的顧客已經等著要解決這個問題很久了。我們希望你了解我們的困境，並且盡早慨然提供50個CPCs讓我們得以結案。

期待你的迅速回覆，謝謝！

誠摯祝福，

安德魯

客戶來信：重點解讀 Getting the Hidden Messages

50個產品是客戶一廂情願的想法，但我方應檢討是否有疏失導致目前的狀況。我方與客戶往來，對客戶有售後服務之責，但對他的顧客並無責任，客戶需自行負起對顧客的承諾，不能賴到我們身上。

客戶是否藉小細故及他的顧客等待賠償為由，而獅子大開口要求50個產品替換？客戶背後真正的目的在於產品的修理替換或使用障眼法目的在於售價的賠償？另外，客戶的說法合理嗎？工程師不會修理，全部要換掉？

攻守之鑰：建立、確認及保留證據
Key Steps: Building, Confirming, and Keeping Evidence

透過電話溝通的交易，除非有電話錄音，否則需要馬上寫一封郵件給客人，確認電話中討論的內容是否正確。現代的交易，不是只有單純的郵件往來，溝通管道也會透過電話及電腦通訊軟體或手機APP（例如Skype、QQ、Line、What's APP……），無論業務老手或新人一定要做到整理保存各種管道溝通的訊息，才不會因為無憑無據而吃悶虧。

對於電話或通訊軟體的即時應答更需小心謹慎，狀況不明下，除了稟告主管及要對方寄來詳細的照片資料了解狀況外，多說可能多錯，當然也不可答應任何求償。

▶ 語言陷阱 Language Traps:

1. We need your conclusion on sending us 50 pieces of CPCs as replacement.

   我們需要你為替換50個CPCs做個結論。

2. It's been over four months since we pointed out this problem to you at the office in person.

   自從我們在辦公室親自向你指出這個問題到現在已經四個多月了。

3. We have already talked on the phone and on your visit about this matter.

   我們已經在電話中以及你來訪的時候討論過這件事。

4. As you know, our customers are waiting for the solution to solve the problem for a long time.

   你知道我們的顧客已經等著要解決這個問題很久了。

5. We hope that you understand our difficult situation and kindly assist us as soon as possible to provide the 50 pieces of CPCs to close the case.

   我們希望你了解我們的困境,並且盡早慨然提供50個CPCs讓我們得以結案。

▶ 技法字詞 Tricky Words and Phrases:

replacement (n.) 替換

solution (n.) 解決

close the case 結案

新手任務 Your Mission:

你該怎麼回？

試寫Now You Try: 請試寫於下方

（試寫後才翻頁）

教戰守則 Insider Tips

　　我方回封短信，表示信中陳述與事實不符。先不要多解釋，也許客戶正在氣頭上。記住無論客戶錯得多離譜（無論是故意錯或是無心錯，請見「先備知識寶典」第6點客訴處理），絕對不能指責客人說錯，引起情緒問題反而模糊問題的焦點。

● 信件範例 Sample Letter:

我方發信給客戶 Our Email to the Client

Dear Andrew,

　　Your email does not conform with fact at the meeting in your office.

　　Best,

　　Reese

親愛的安德魯：

　　你的電郵與你的辦公室會議事實不符。

　　誠摯祝福，

　　瑞絲

▶ 關鍵字詞 Key Words and Phrases:

　　not conform with fact 與事實不符

客戶來電

上封信回覆幾天後,客戶不理會我們的回覆內容,工程師撥電話來說明產品不良原因,並繼續索賠。

● 新手任務 Your Mission:

客戶打電話來繼續要求不存在的「共識」,你如何解套?

● 試寫Now You Try: 請試寫於下方

（試寫後才翻頁）

錯誤發生在我方業務當時沒有在最短的時間內把電話內容寫成文字紀錄郵寄給客人及他的工程師，想從不利局勢解套，全然不給客戶一些回饋必定遭致反彈，為求損失降低及彼此繼續合作，必須應允給予少數新品替換。

▶ 語言祕訣 Language Tips:

1. 表達不同意

There is **no agreement on** the 50 pieces of CPCs replacement.
我們沒有同意50臺CPCs的替換品。

2. 表達震驚

Free replacement of 50 pieces of CPCs was **unimaginable**.
50臺CPCs免費替換是令人無法想像的。

3. 可同意之讓步

After consulting my manager, **we will provide** 5 pieces of CPCs.
跟經理請示後，我們同意提供5臺CPCs。

▶ 關鍵字詞 Key Words and Phrases:

agreement (n.) 同意

unimaginable (adj.) 無法想像的，不合理的

consult (v.) 請示，諮詢

我方發信給客戶 Our Email to the Client

Dear Andrew,

There is no agreement on the 50 pieces of CPCs replacement. On the phone conversation, I said I would report it to my manager because free replacement of 50 pieces of CPCs was unimaginable. After consulting my manager, we will provide 5 pieces of CPCs.

Best,

Reese

親愛的安德魯：

我們沒有同意50臺CPCs的替換品，電話會談我表示會向我的經理報告，因為50臺CPCs免費替換是令人無法想像的，跟經理請示後，我們同意提供5臺CPCs。

誠摯祝福，

瑞絲

Round 3
第三回合

客戶來信 Client's Reply

Dear Reese,

We await your conclusion about the 50 pieces of CPCs.

Thank you.

Best regards,

Andrew

親愛的瑞絲：

我們等待你50臺CPCs的結論。

誠摯祝福，

安德魯

 客戶來信：重點解讀 Getting the Hidden Messages

客人很聰明的來封極短信，完全不回應我們第一封所說「與事實不符」以及第二封的解釋與應允條件，而是緊咬我們50臺貨品就是有問題。

▶ **語言陷阱 Language Traps:**

我們等待你50臺CPCs的結論。

We await your conclusion on the 50 pieces of CPCs.

● **新手任務 Your Mission:**

客戶緊咬50臺的賠償，完全不理我們的前兩封信，你必須還原事實寫出整個經過，回給客戶一封誠懇及與事實相符的信，釐清任何不該被混淆的說詞。

（試寫後才翻頁）

教戰守則 Insider Tips

仔細呈現事實經過，強調商業往來首重信譽，重述可應允提供與上封信相同之條件，做出最小犧牲。

▶ **語言祕訣 Language Tips:**

1. 強調信用

Since **integrity is the foundation** of any long-term business relationship.

信用是所有長期商業關係的根本。

2. 感激與展望

We value your business and regard that we both **strive for a better future**.

我們重視你們的商機，也認為我們雙方都為更好的未來而努力。

3. 重申應允條件（顯示我方信用）

If there are defects, **we will issue** spare parts or a credit note to your company.

如有瑕疵貨物，我們會提供備用零件或信用額度給貴公司。

4. 說明待釐清事由

To prevent any misunderstanding, **we must clarify a few things**.

避免任何誤解，我們要釐清一些事。

5. 會議已確認技師資格

In the meeting, we also **verified** the Chinese technician Mr.

Min Lee's **qualification** on fixing the products.

在會議中，我們也確認了中國技師李明先生有能力修理產品。

6. 對照今技師無技術（暗示無信用）

Unexpectedly, now Mr. Min Lee cannot repair the products and claims that the 50 pieces to be replaced.

出乎意料地，現在李明先生無法修理產品，並且表示50個產品都要替換。

7. 提出我方數據

We have always kept our defect rate under 1-3% in our over 50 years of business history.

在我們五十多年的歷史中，瑕疵率總是控制在1-3%之間。

8. 不接受不合理之要求

Asking for the entire 50 pieces of replacement before any product selling is **simply unacceptable**.

在售出任何產品前就要求50個替換品我們完全不能接受。

9. 再次強調

We must emphasize again that the situation is unacceptable.

我們必須再次強調，這個情況我們是無法接受的。

10. 彼此合作才有機會

Only by working better together can we have better business opportunities in the future.

只有更好的合作，將來我們才有更好的機會。

integrity (n.) 正直，誠信

credit note 信用額度

clarify (v.) 釐清

verify (v.) 確認

qualification (n.) 資格

defect rate 瑕疵率

● 信件範例 Sample Letter:

我方發信給客戶 Our Email to the Client

Dear Andrew,

In our last mail, we have given you the conclusion:

We will provide 5 pieces of CPCs.

Since integrity is the foundation of any long-term business relationship, we value your business and regard that we both strive for a better future. If there are defects, we will issue spare parts or a credit note to your company.

To prevent any misunderstanding, we must clarify a few things. In the meeting, we did agree to provide 2-3 pieces of CPCs for replacement. We also verified the Chinese technician Mr. Min Lee's qualification on fixing the products. Mr. Min Lee reassured his adequacy because it was the reason that he could work in Singapore.

Unexpectedly, now Mr. Min Lee cannot repair the products and claims that the 50 pieces to be replaced. We cannot accept such an unthinkable result because we have always kept our defect rate under

1-3% in our over 50 years of business history. Asking for the entire 50 pieces of replacement before any product selling is simply unacceptable. We must emphasize again that the situation is unacceptable.

Even though we are faced the dreadful experience, it is our hope to grow from it. To resolve the situation, we will provide

1. 5 pieces of CPCs
2. caps for your future maintenance.

For any customer service cases in the future, it is necessary that you provide pictures and product serial numbers for us to identify problems. Only by working better together can we have better business opportunities in the future.

Best regards,
Reese

親愛的安德魯：

上封郵件裡，我們已經給你們結論：我們會提供5個CPCs。

因為信用是所有長期商業關係的根本，我們重視你們的商機，也認為我們雙方都為更好的未來而努力。因此，如有瑕疵貨物，我們會提供備用零件或信用額度給貴公司。

為了避免任何誤解，我們要釐清一些事。會議中我們確實同意提供2-3臺CPCs給你們替換。在會議中，我們也確認了中國技師李明先生有能力修理產品。李明先生再次保證他有足夠資格，這是他得以在新加坡工作的原因。

出乎意料地，現在李明先生無法修理產品，並且表示50個產品都要替換。我們無法接受這樣難以置信的結果，因為在我們50多年的歷史中，瑕疵率總是控制在1-3%之間。在售出任何產品前就要求50個替

換品我們完全不能接受。我們必須再次強調，這個情況我們是無法接受的。

既使我們面對這樣的遭遇，我們仍抱著從經驗中成長的希望。爲了解決這樣的情況，我們會提供

1. 5個CPCs

2. 爲你們將來的維修提供產品的帽蓋。

將來的任何售後服務，你們必須提供照片及產品序號讓我們能辨識問題所在。只有更好的合作，將來我們才有更好的機會。

誠摯祝福，

瑞絲

Round 4
第四回合

客戶回信 Client's Reply

Dear Reese,

We will get back to you after a company meeting regarding this case. Our point is on compensation, in cash.

Best,

Andrew

親愛的瑞絲：

關於這個案子，我們內部開會後會回覆你，我們的重點在於賠償，以現金的方式賠償。

誠摯祝福，

安德魯

客戶來信：重點解讀 Getting the Hidden Messages

客戶又在下筆新訂單，留一手了！

▶ **語言陷阱 Language Traps:**

1. We will get back to you after a company meeting regarding this case.
   關於這個案子，我們內部開會後會回覆你。

2. Our point is on compensation, in cash.
   我們的重點在於賠償，以現金的方式賠償。

▶ **技法字詞 Tricky Words and Phrases:**

point (n.) 重點

compensation (n.) 賠償

in cash 現金

💬 **新手任務 Your Mission:**

面對這樣的客戶，如何脫困？

💬 **試寫Now You Try:** 請試寫於下方

_____

_____

_____

_____

_____

（試寫後才翻頁）

教戰守則 Insider Tips

重申立場。

▶ **語言祕訣 Language Tips:**

重申同意給予之條件

We do not agree to provide cash, but as mentioned in our previous mail **we can provide**...

我們不同意提供現金，但可以提供如上封信所提之……

信件範例 Sample Letter:

我方發信給客戶 Our Email to the Client

Dear Andrew,

We do not agree to provide cash, but as mentioned in our previous mail we can provide

1. 5 pieces of CPCs

2. caps for your future maintenance.

Best regards,

Reese

親愛的安德魯：

我們不同意提供現金，但可以提供上封信所提之

1. 5個CPCs

2. 為你們將來的維修提供產品的帽蓋。

誠摯祝福，

瑞絲

▶ 關鍵字詞 Key Words and Phrases:

caps (n.) 帽蓋

future maintenance 將來維修

★★★★★★★★★★★★★★★目標達成★★★★★★★★★★★★★★★

攻防4回合後，客戶未再來信要現金賠償，半年後又下訂單，持續生意往來。

擴大合作規模
Expanding Business Cooperation

臺灣LH集團 vs 美國MOTOR MASTER公司

客戶與案例背景說明
Background of the Client and the Case

客戶爲《華爾街日報》推薦美國成長最快中小企業之一，近期獲得投資公司資金挹注，該公司爲擴大營業規模及項目，特別安排優先供應廠商（priority supplier）至美國該公司開會。

會議由國際採購經理主持，約四十多歲，美國中部知名大學商學院畢（非技術科系）。參加會議者包含副總裁（Vice Chairman, VC），運輸及倉庫部主管、技術開發部主管、採購部助理，但財務部主管未參加。

出國開會前之準備

出國開會可能是一場硬仗，你預期開會流程爲何？需要什麼準備？如果你的主管交代你準備出國用的會議資料，你要準備什麼呢？

1. **心理與體力準備**

   到國外開會可說身在敵營，主場優勢不在我方，長途飛行時差問題尚未克服，加上自行開車前往，體力、腦力、資源、開會語言都處於不利地位，對方如爲大企業，部門主管多，一字排開，可說陣仗驚人，但我方人員出差時間與預算有

限，主管經常單槍匹馬赴會，或最多兩三人，各條件不對等情形下，心理與體力準備尤為重要。

開會可能一天或數天，客戶安排的開會順序大約如下，各主管輪番上陣：

(1) 採購部門主管。

(2) 品質部門主管（與會目的如要向我方索賠，我方要有工程師與會）。

(3) 倉管（含包裝）部門主管（與會目的同樣為索賠）。

(4) 業務部門主管（與會目的為增加新產品項目，或聯合以上部門，彼此助陣為砍價）。

(5) 財務部門主管（與會目的為對帳，可能雙方五分鐘就核對完，簽字確認）。

    i. 如雙方付款條件不做記帳（O/A），財務部門主管通常不會出現；若突然出現，可能客戶要更改付款條件了。

    ii. 如果雙方付款條件做記帳（O/A），財務沒出現，就無法對帳。我方大老遠飛去，卻無法完成僅僅幾分鐘，但對我方最重要的財務工作。

(6) 若有法務部門法律團隊出現，可能要買保險或準備上法院了，也有可能要簽新合約或換合約。

(7) 若對方為製造商（有技術開發部），我方要帶工程師，開會可能一天或數天，工程師到時出現即可。

無論開會一天或數天，皆需有體力及心理消耗戰之準備，經常在你最累的時候，也就是迎接最關鍵挑戰（財務或法務）的時候。對付時差及體力、腦力疲憊，甚至多雪及溫差，每個人的方法可能不同，但開會當下吃大量高糖、高熱量食物，不受飢餓或低血糖能量不足之困擾，也是可行辦法之一。

2. **資料準備**

(1) 開會人員有誰（我方／對方），是否須派工程師？

(2) 現在買哪些產品？

(3) 我們要推薦哪些產品？

(4) 近三年採購的營業額及產品項目之消長圖。

(5) 客訴紀錄（項目及解決後客戶是否滿意）。

(6) 生產及交貨狀況。

(7) 近期原物料價格成本。

Round 1
第一回合

新手任務 Your Mission:

新手接到任務要準備主管出國開會資料，新手還要準備什麼讓老闆刮目相看？

試寫Now You Try: 請試寫於下方

（試寫後才翻頁）

教戰守則 Insider Tips

你的準備功夫關係會議成敗：

1. 預期會議討論重點，準備所需數據及單據。
2. 自備國外數據連線，任何情況下都不要使用客戶wifi，以避免公司資料遭竊。買賣雙方開會本來就是諜對諜！
3. 為避免連不上線無法讀取公司網頁或資料，先行下載或擷取頁面存檔。
4. 當場錄音及做會議紀錄，會議中回答主管問你的確切數據。
5. 會議結束盡快完成會議紀錄，請主管過目補正。

信件範例 Sample Letter:

我方發信給客戶 Our Email to the Client

Dear Rod,

　　Would it be possible to meet you at your office on Aug. 10 (Wed.) at 10 a.m.?

　　Best regards,

　　Sophie

親愛的羅德：

　　8月10日（三）早上10點能在你辦公室會面嗎？

　　誠摯祝福，

　　蘇菲

 ## 客戶回信 Client's Reply

> Dear Sophie,
>
> I am sorry that I won't be available on Aug. 10. Our staff could welcome you. However, I surely would hope to meet you in the office on Aug. 9 or 11. Please advise if either of the dates is possible for you. Sorry again for causing your inconvenience.
>
> Rod
>
> Purchasing Manager

親愛的蘇菲：

很抱歉8月10日我不在辦公室，我們的同仁可以接待你。但是我很希望能夠跟你在8月9日或11日在辦公室見面。請告知其中一天你是否有可能，再次抱歉造成你不方便。

羅德

採購經理

 ## 客戶來信：重點解讀 Getting the Hidden Messages

客戶強烈表示要見面！我們就要自己想辦法配合日期，包括改機票，當然這客戶必須極具潛力。

▶ **客戶用語表達Client's Expressions:**

Our staff could welcome you. However, I surely would hope to meet you in the office.

我們的同仁可以接待你，但是我很希望能夠跟你在辦公室見面。

Round 2
第二回合

💬 信件範例 Sample Letter:

♞ 我方回信 Our Email to the Client（經理親回）

Dear Rod,

　　Thank you for your reply; we can meet you in your office on Aug. 9 (Tue.) at 10 a.m.

　　Thank you.

　　Best regards,

　　Sophie

親愛的羅德：

　　謝謝你的回覆，我們可以跟你在8月9日（星期二）早上10點在你的辦公室見面。

　　謝謝！

　　誠摯祝福，

　　蘇菲

♞ 客戶回信 Client's Reply

Dear Sophie,

　　Thanks for being so flexible--Aug. 9 (Tue.) at 10 a.m. Do you need transportation arrangements?

　　Have a great day!

　　Rod

親愛的蘇菲：

　　謝謝你這麼有彈性──8月9日（二）早上10點。你們需要交通安排嗎？

　　祝你有很棒的一天！

　　羅德

 ## 客戶來信：重點解讀 Getting the Hidden Messages

　　客戶表面上體貼的詢問「你是否需要交通的安排？」，事實上是要了解你的交通方式，「你搭機還是開車過來？」如果你開車，表示你可能在當地還有客戶。其他的問題如「你這次拜訪的時間多久？」、「你的下一站是哪裡？」、「你會去哪些城市？」、「你要開車過去嗎？」、「進入芝加哥可是會大塞車的。」、「你在美國還有哪些客戶？」、「你的產品賣給誰？」、「會議結束後，要載你到機場嗎？」等等。任何你的回答都可以讓客戶推測你出差的路線或動態，客戶問這些看起來是關心你、為你設想的問題，背後其實是想知己知彼，防止你有益於他的競爭對手，而影響到他的利益。

▶ 語言陷阱 Language Traps:

Do you need transportation arrangements?
你需要交通安排嗎？

▶ 其他打探動向的語句

1. How long are you visiting?
   你這次拜訪的時間多久？

2. What is your next stop?
   你的下一站是哪裡？

3. Are you going to visit other cities?
   你會拜訪其他城市嗎？

4. Are you going to the airport after the meeting?
   會議結束後，你要去機場嗎？

5. What other cities are you visiting this time?
   你這次要拜訪哪些城市？

6. Who are you selling to?
   你的產品賣給誰？

7. What other clients do you have in the US?
   你在美國還有哪些客戶？

▶ 技法字詞 Tricky Words and Phrases:

transportation arrangements 交通安排

Round 3
第三回合

● 新手任務 Your Mission:

　　經理可能要你回信，如果客戶問你其他關於動向的問題，你該如何回答？

● 試寫Now You Try: 請試寫於下方

_____

_____

_____

_____

（試寫後才翻頁）

教戰守則 Insider Tips

　　自己開車去見客戶，表示在美國有行動自由，可能有其他客戶，此客戶不是唯一。這樣的交通方式會引發客戶的打探，想弄清楚他究竟有何競爭對手，處於何種競爭狀況。

▶ **語言祕訣 Language Tips:**

表達有移動力

I have already booked a rental car.
我已經預約租車了。

信件範例 Sample Letter:

我方發信給客戶 Our Email to the Client

Dear Rod,

　　We have already booked a rental car. See you next Tuesday.

　　Have a great weekend!

　　Best regards,

　　Sophie

親愛的羅德：

　　我們已經預約租車了，下週二見。

　　週末愉快！

　　誠摯祝福，

　　蘇菲

客戶回信 Client's Reply

> Sophie,
>
> How long is your intended visit? Are you flying out the same day?
>
> Best,
>
> Rod

蘇菲：

你預計會面的時間多久？是否當天就搭機離開？

誠摯祝福，

羅德

 客戶來信：重點解讀 Getting the Hidden Messages

果不其然，客戶的問題完全如我們所料。

Round 4
第四回合

● 新手任務 Your Mission:

若客戶把時間的主控權給我們，我們該盡可能給客戶時間嗎？

● 試寫Now You Try: 請試寫於下方

（試寫後才翻頁）

教戰守則 Insider Tips

雖然出國拜訪客戶一次不容易，但時間安排要以客戶為重。如果客人給我們一整天時間，就要帶工程師（除非業務對產品非常了解可以排除產品不良的困難），如果只有兩三個小時，就不一定要帶工程師。

若客戶禮貌性地把時間的主控權給我們，我們的回答就要聰明，記住要對我們有利，給自己保留彈性，最後當然是要顧及禮貌。我們必須預計彼此可能談話的重點，時間夠討論重點就好，給太多時間對我們反而不利。如果回答「a whole day」，將失去以時間為藉口離開的先機。

▶ 語言祕訣 Language Tips:

控制時間

If necessary, we can have a few hours to discuss business.
如果必要的話，我們可以討論幾個小時。

● 信件範例 Sample Letter:

我方發信給客戶 Our Email to the Client

> Dear Rod,
>
> If necessary, we can have a few hours to discuss business.
>
> Thanks.
>
> Sophie

親愛的羅德：

如果必要的話，我們可以討論幾個小時。

謝謝！

蘇菲

客戶回信 Client's Reply

> Sophie,
>
> Ok. Thank you. We will plan on lunch together.
>
> Rod

蘇菲：

好的，謝謝。我們計畫一起午餐。

羅德

Round 5
第五回合

我們準備見面要談的重點，並預測對方的問題。此時，客戶來信了。

客戶來信 Client's Letter

> Sophie,
>
> To make our discussion as constructive as possible, please see the following key p...oints we prepare.
>
> 1. Your entire production process: from the beginning to the end
> 2. The entire quality control process: How product quality is checked? How often? How many times? Can you show us the steps?
> 3. Your packaging system and materials
> 4. Your current production capacity
> 5. Your increasing capacity in the future: How do you plan to increase capacity if we increase growth together?

6. The possibility of reducing 5-10% of our cost: what can we do?

We earnestly look forward to meeting you and understanding your business more so we can continue to grow together.

Thank you and have a great day!

Rod

蘇菲：

為了讓我們的討論有建設性，請看我們準備的要點如下：

1. 你們的整個生產流程：從頭到尾
2. 整個品質控制流程：產品品質怎麼檢查？頻率？次數？可以給我們看步驟嗎？
3. 包裝系統跟材質
4. 現今的產能
5. 將來的產能：如果我們一起成長，你們計畫如何增加產能？
6. 降低我們成本5-10%的可能性，我們能做什麼？

我們誠摯地盼望跟你會面，並多多了解你們的企業，如此我們可以一起繼續成長。

謝謝你，祝福你有美好的一天！

羅德

 客戶來信：重點解讀 Getting the Hidden Messages

「please see the following key p...oints we prepare.」看到不尋常的 p...oints，可見他強調提出的這幾點有多重要。六個重點看起來龐雜，我們赴會前必須一一拆解歸納這些重點，才能看穿究竟客戶想要什麼？

● 新手任務 Your Mission:

你整理看看，能不能把重點弄成簡單扼要些？

● 試寫Now You Try: 請試寫於下方

_____

_____

_____

_____

_____

_____

_____

_____

_____

_____

_____

_____

_____

_____

_____

_____

（試寫後才翻頁）

▶ 語言陷阱 Language Traps:

1. Your entire production process: from the beginning to the end

   注意到了嗎？交貨時間（lead time）才是重點，也就是從客戶下單到生產完成可以交貨所需的時間，重點並不是生產流程（production process）。這點其實省略了幾個字How long does it take to...，客戶這麼問是想要讓你多說獲得資訊。

2. The entire quality control process: How product quality is checked? How often? How many times? Can you show us the steps?

   注意到了嗎？重點字是quality，不是process。

3. Your packaging system and materials

   注意到了嗎？重點還是quality，不是packaging system如何。

4. Your current production capacity

   注意到了嗎？重點是交貨時間lead time。

5. Your increasing capacity in the future: How do you plan to increase capacity if we increase growth together?

   注意到了嗎？重點還是交貨時間lead time。

6. The possibility of reducing 5-10% of our cost: what can we do?

   這你一定看得懂，重點是價格，談錢傷感情，卻是最大關鍵，所以放在最後壓軸。

歸納好之後，我們發現客戶寫的一長串，真正的重點只有三個：

1. 交貨時間lead time

2. 品質控制quality control

3. 價格price

客戶不是唐突地硬生生只要求降價，而是說我們彼此能做什麼？

這當然可能是表面話，重點是「你」要做，而不是他要做。

客戶雖是主人，我們開會的時候要被這些他列出來的「重點」以及他鋪陳的順序牽著鼻子走嗎？你必然在想那結果會怎麼樣？會議既然是雙方的，當然雙方都希望會議圓滿，並且達到自己的預期利益。一方面我們不希望被牽著鼻子走，而我們也已經整理出來客戶想要的三個重點，那麼開會前的準備該怎麼做？我們該在何時配合演出？何時拿回我們的主軸？

Round 6
第六回合

🗨 新手任務 Your Mission:

　　詢問主管或老闆預計會議如何進行？客戶可能問的尖銳問題是什麼？我方該如何因應？我們是否在赴會前要整理出客戶想知道的三個重點（交貨時間、品質、價格）？是否客戶要我們答我們就答？我們是否在回答前，要從客戶那裡問到什麼訊息，才能回答這些重點？

🗨 試寫Now You Try: 請試寫於下方

（試寫後才翻頁）

　　雖然在客戶的地盤開會，對方可能派出各部門主管，假若我們只有單槍匹馬或兩人，可說寡不敵眾，如能掌握會議進行的主動權，才可對我方有利。客戶在最後一刻才拋出要你在會議回答的一串問題，不要因為輕忽、時間來不及或時差疲倦而配合對方，以客戶列出的問題為會議的議程而被牽著鼻子走。

　　國外客戶不會關心你的時差，會議本身就是攻防戰，長途飛行的舟車勞頓，加上開車找路前往的時差勞累，他們輕易在思緒及體力上就可以占上風。如果客戶要你解釋製作流程，你照著做反而不利，因為解釋愈多，客戶愈能挑你毛病。最好的方式是讓他講或問，你不要細講，而是用統整的方式回答。無論如何，你都必須在會議前整理出有利我方的作法。

▶ **語言祕訣 Language Tips:**

　　我方在會議前一刻簡要整理出三個客戶關切的重點，這也是我們最關切的。但我們不能直接回答客戶的問題，而是要請他們先回答我們關於這三點的問題（我們須先準備好，在會議裡以電腦螢幕或書面〔非口頭〕出示這些問題，使他們按照這個順序回答），有了客戶的答案後，我們才能回答客戶的問題。這三點的順序不能隨意，而是按照重點邏輯安排：

1. **LEAD TIME (ON TIME DELIVERY) 交貨時間（準時遞送）**
   我們要先回答，才能問預計採購量多寡及銷售額，以及客戶對該產品之未來計畫。

2. **QUALITY CONTROL 品質控制**
   賣到美國消費者手上一年，因為不知客戶何時出售給消費

者，通常提供給客人保固時間為貨到客人手上一年三個月到
六個月，即客人有在三到六個月一定要售出的時間壓力。

3. PRICE 價格

留到最後，等該說的都說了之後，再談價錢。不要直接回答
降價多少，而要用有趣的方式反問。

給客戶的問題列出如下：

1. 將來你們會增加多少採購量？明年呢？（量跟價相關）

How much quantity will be increased in the future? Next year?
(Quantity and price are related.)

2. 你們希望的交貨時間多久？你們的銷售額會決定交貨時間
（銷售快，交貨就快）。

How long do you wish for your lead time? Your sales decide the
lead time.

3. 關於我們的品質，你們的問題及關切點是什麼？或是你們有
任何想法？

What are your questions or concerns about our quality? Or do
you have any ideas about our quality?

4. 我們希望跟你們增加生意，如何合作才能增加雙方的利益？

We hope to increase business with you. How do we cooperate to
increase mutual benefits?

（最後他們問我們增加雙方利益的問題，也同樣是我們要問
他們的問題。）

5. 價格方面，你們最理想的價格是什麼？

About price: what's your sweet spot?

mutual benefits 雙方的利益，互惠

sweet spot 甜區（棒球之有效打擊點）

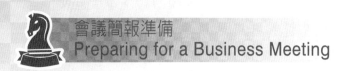

會議簡報準備
Preparing for a Business Meeting

● 新手任務 Your Mission:

你要準備哪些重點？介紹哪些產品？要注意什麼？要準備什麼圖表？除了簡報外，你還擔任會議紀錄跟主管的翻譯，一定要準備好將會議內容錄音，以備往後查證之用。

● 試寫Now You Try: 請試寫於下方

（試寫後才翻頁）

會前先了解有多少時間拜訪，作為簡報時間依據。與老闆討論（會前會）可以給客戶的付款條件，簡報準備重點依是否初次會面而定。

▶ 如雙方「初次」會面

1. **公司歷史簡介**

   介紹給客戶的產品，不是自己隨意挑，而要參考對方網頁，挑選對方有興趣及有在販售的產品，顯示考慮對方需求，為對方著想。想要推動的產品放在後面，不要意圖太明顯，反而會弄巧成拙。

2. **介紹生產線，生產量（工廠為一班、兩班或三班運轉），是否擴廠？客戶如非進口商而是工廠，要小心，不要亂開支票，要實事求是。**

3. **全程之品質管制（from start to finish）**

   (1) 客戶如為進口商，客人詢問重點為是否有進口標準。

   (2) 客戶如為工廠，必須詳細介紹每個過程（零件、生產組合、包裝、使用者反饋）之良率。如能提出業界良率更好，一定要有確切的數字才可。然而，如此詳細介紹效果一體兩面，買主很精明的話，我方可能傷到自己。如果我們良率很好，客戶必然會問如何保持良率，我們可以據實回答（例如：員工訓練、經度校正等）。

4. **交貨時間（lead time）**

   問客戶預計採購量。

5. **價格談判：付款條件與報價條件**

   (1) 問客戶希望如何付款。

   (2) 客戶可能提出出貨以後120天（OA/120 days）OA/TT 30%訂金，出貨前付完餘款（承兌交單DA），或是採用第三方支付（即付款交單DP），客戶取文件時付款。

   (3) 要問對方報價條件（對方可能已與你討論過），因為報價條件關係到貨物未收到款時的權利。

▶ **非首次會面**

簡報除了給我們看，也是做給雙方公司開會成員看（例如：客戶希望擴大規模時，簡報會介紹公司歷史及我們產品的銷售狀況。我方簡報也會包含公司歷史，產品問題解決迅速等內容。一來呈現給雙方人員了解，二來意在期望將來繼續保持）。

專心做會議紀錄，不明白的地方等會後問主管，記住雙方開會就是諜對諜場合，即使目的是彼此合作，絕對不可在會議間，浪費客戶時間，還可能造成更多問題。

會議結束後，雙方可能會互要對方開會時的簡報做參考（會後分析對方簡報）。離開前禮貌道別（It was a pleasure meeting you.）使雙方對會議留下好印象（to leave on a good note），有利下一步的合作及溝通。

Round 7
第七回合

💬 **新手任務 Your Mission:**

會議結束後，你必須在最短時間內完成會議紀錄給主管過目。你要怎麼斟酌立場及用字？

● 試寫Now You Try: 請試寫於下方

（試寫後才翻頁）

教戰守則 Insider Tips

掌握會議紀錄即主動掌握發語權。如果單槍匹馬赴會，我方無人記錄，幾乎註定吃虧。人員隨行記錄，切記一定要錄音，開會前就向對方說明有錄音需求，以作為記錄完整之用。

會議紀錄撰寫原則如下：

1. 會議紀錄為正式文件，包含雙方公司名稱、會議時間、場地及參與人員。頭尾須有公司表頭、紀錄執筆者及頁碼編號。

2. 內容：以分類條例方式列出會議討論後重點。既然由我方執筆，當然須寫出對於我方有利的重點跟立場，對於我方不利的情形要弱化，使用之措辭須增大我方迴旋之空間。

3. 記得附上雙方在會議中向對方要求之資料或樣品。

4. 何時寄出：思慮完備後，愈快寄出愈好（以PDF檔寄送）。如雙方同時記錄，先寄出者贏，如幾乎同時寄出，雙方就彼此差異點作回應。如須釐清任何爭議，有錄音才有依據作為解決之道。

5. 對方如有修改，我方回應須字字斟酌，不需匆忙！

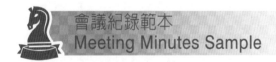

會議紀錄範本
Meeting Minutes Sample

Meeting Minutes for Motor Master and LH
8/9/2016 (T) 10 a.m.-1 p.m.
Location: Motor Master Conference Room
Participants--Motor Master: Rod Wilson, Gary Smith, Sarah Jones
LH: Frank Lin, Sophie Wong

1. LH appreciate your business to participate in your fast and strong growth.

2. Could you please send us the PPT at the meeting for LH staff to better understand Motor Master?

3. For Rod's information, the points LH mentioned at the meeting are listed below.

4. Special thanks to Gary for introducing the BEAM System for LH to learn the concept.

PRODUCTS

1. LH will introduce new products for Motor Master to check over first.

2. Products that are designed or modified by Motor Master will be exclusively sold by Motor Master.

3. LH will support Motor Master much ahead of a product life cycle in the market.

4. LH will extend the product life cycle by varying accessories or adding the product's functions.

5. LH has many patents. Please notify us for any similar or pirated goods to protect our long-term mutual benefits. In such case, please introduce attorneys for LH.

6. LH will provide one sample for MO BASE3800 and newly designed MO PRO5800.

7. Motor Master can accept prototypes from LH and give feedback in return.

8. Motor Master will provide the distance from the rear tire to the kick stand and the pad size of the kick stand.

TWO CHANGES ABOUT PRODUCTS TO BE MADE.

1. The base of the KC1055 packaging should be two inches high.

2. The space for KC1057 should be 38-42 inches.

QUALITY

1. To ensure quality, LH will adopt a camera image matching system for better quality control.

2. LH has ISO standards and has formed a quality control system in China. Despite challenges from educating the Chinese workers, to always improve quality to the best is our goal.

FUTURE GROWTH

1. LH and Motor Master will strengthen the ability to reduce the risk from any unpredictable events (e.g., G20). Motor Master will provide half of a year forecast and fulfill at least 70% of sales.

2. LH can provide Motor Master warehouse in Shanghai to consolidate various products to reduce Motor Master sales risks.

3. In the future, LH and Motor Master can cooperate to sell products in China or have products go global.

FOR ROD'S INFORMATION

From your mail, we summarize three key points.

1. Lead time (on time delivery)

2. Quality control

3. Price

We need to get some key information before answering your questions:

1. How much quantity will be increased in the future or next year?

2. How long do you wish for your lead time?

3. What are your questions or concerns about our quality? Or do you

have any ideas about our quality?

4. We hope to increase business with you. How do we cooperate to increase mutual benefits?

5. About price: what is your sweet spot?

 客戶更正會議紀錄

客戶主管（Gary）可能會先回覆一兩個更正或疑問，再由下方負責主管（Rod）仔細逐項回覆。一來主管先向我們禮貌知會收到，下方負責主管也可以有些時間討論再回覆。範例中客戶主管Gary回覆更正須改變項目第二點之尺寸，我們將會議紀錄該點更正後（畫底線顯示更正處），寄給客戶（PDF檔）命名爲「最終版」，希望Rod不要再有更多註解。中文請見下頁含對方逐項回覆意見之「最終版會議紀錄」。

Meeting Minutes (FINALIZED) for Motor Master and LH

8/9/2016 (T) 10 a.m.-1 p.m. (REVISED 8/11/2016)

Location: Motor Master Conference Room

Participants--Motor Master: Rod Wilson, Gary Smith, Sarah Jones

LH: Frank Lin, Sophie Wong

1. LH appreciate your business to participate in your fast and strong growth.

2. Could you please send us the PPT at the meeting for LH staff to better understand Motor Master?

3. For Rod's information, the points LH mentioned at the meeting are listed below.

4. Special thanks to Gary for introducing the BEAM System for LH

to learn the concept.

PRODUCTS

1. LH will introduce new products for Motor Master to check over first.
2. Products that are designed or modified by Motor Master will be exclusively sold by Motor Master.
3. LH will support Motor Master much ahead of a product life cycle in the market.
4. LH will extend the product life cycle by varying accessories or adding the product's functions.
5. LH has many patents. Please notify us for any similar or pirated goods to protect our long-term mutual benefits. In such case, please introduce attorneys for LH.
6. LH will provide one sample for MO BASE3800 and newly designed MO PRO5800.
7. Motor Master can accept prototypes from LH and give feedback in return.
8. Motor Master will provide the distance from the rear tire to the kick stand and the pad size of the kick stand.

TWO CHANGES ABOUT PRODUCTS TO BE MADE.

1. The heel of wood packaging should be two inches high.
2. The width of the space for fork lift should be NO LESS than 36 inches, and NO MORE than 44 inches.

QUALITY

1. To ensure quality, LH will adopt a camera image matching system for better quality control.
2. LH has ISO standards and has formed a quality control system in

China. Despite challenges from educating the Chinese workers, to always improve quality to the best is our goal.

FUTURE GROWTH

1. LH and Motor Master will strengthen the ability to reduce the risk from any unpredictable events (e.g., G20). Motor Master will provide half of a year forecast and fulfill at least 70% of sales.

2. LH can provide Motor Master warehouse in Shanghai to consolidate various products to reduce Motor Master sales risks.

3. In the future, LH and Motor Master can cooperate to sell products in China or have products go global.

FOR ROD'S INFORMATION

From your mail, we summarize three key points.

1. Lead time (on time delivery)

2. Quality control

3. Price

We need to get some key information before answering your questions:

1. About price: what is your sweet spot?

2. How much quantity will be increased in the future or next year?

3. How long do you wish for your lead time?

4. What are your questions or concerns about our quality? Or do you have any ideas about our quality?

5. We hope to increase business with you. How do we cooperate to increase mutual benefits?

在會議結束後，要請對方寄給我們會議時他們的簡報，因在對方簡報時我們必須聆聽回應，可能忽略對方之順序鋪陳。回顧檢討使我們在會議結束後，再度從簡報中了解客戶簡報的順序及目的，盼能見樹又見

林，以檢視我們會前是否做好攻防預備，評估參與會議時我方掌握情勢之能力，作為將來改進。

♞ 客戶回信 Client's Reply

在客戶主管Gary回覆後，而我們也寄回含有他註解之最終版會議紀錄後，負責的部門主管Rod寄來詳細的逐項回覆（斜體標示）。

Meeting Minutes (FINALIZED) for Motor Master and LH
8/9/2016 (T) 10 a.m.-1 p.m. (REVISED 8/11/2016)
Location: Motor Master Conference Room
Participants--Motor Master: Rod Wilson, Gary Smith, Sarah Jones
LH: Frank Lin, Sophie Wong

1. LH appreciate your business to participate in your fast and strong growth. *We also appreciate your partnership.*
   LH感激能參與貴公司的快速穩健的成長。*我們也感激你們的夥伴關係。*

2. Could you please send us the PPT at the meeting for LH staff to better understand Motor Master? *Yes, see attachment.*
   是否能寄給我們會議中的投影片讓LH員工多了解Motor Master？*好，如附件。*

3. For Rod's information, the points LH mentioned at the meeting are listed below. *Thank you.*
   羅德需要的資訊，LH在會中所提列之各點在下方。*謝謝。*

4. Special thanks to Gary for introducing the BEAM System for LH to learn the concept. *Gary surely has ideas and experience. We are learning from you too. Together we can go stronger.*

特別感謝蓋瑞介紹BEAM系統讓LH了解此概念。*蓋瑞確實有想法跟經驗，我們也向你們學習，我們可以一起變得更強。*

PRODUCTS 產品

1. LH will introduce new products for Motor Master to check over first. *Thank you. We will be the leader in sales for your goods.*
   LH會優先介紹新產品給Motor Master檢視。*謝謝，我們會成為你們產品的領導者。*

2. Products that are designed or modified by Motor Master will be exclusively sold by Motor Master. *Thank you, but we are still disappointed that we did not get the first chance to sale MO1157.*
   為Motor Master設計或修正的產品會給Motor Master獨家專賣。*謝謝，但我們對於沒能首賣MO1157還是很失望。*

3. LH will support Motor Master much ahead of a product life cycle in the market. *Yes, as our business has planned and proven.*
   LH會支持Motor Master領先產品在市場上的生命週期。*是的，如我們所規劃並已證明。*

4. LH will extend the product life cycle by varying accessories or adding the product's functions. *Great, as discussed.*
   LH會以增加產品配件或增加產品功能來延長產品的生命週期。*很好，如我們的討論結果。*

5. LH has many patents. Please notify us for any similar or pirated goods to protect our long-term mutual benefits. In such case, please introduce attorneys for LH. *Yes, see attachment.*
   LH有許多專利，請通知我們任何相同或仿冒的產品，以保護我們雙方的長期利益。如果真有發生，請介紹律師給我們。*好的，請看附件。*

6. LH will provide one sample for MO BASE3800 and newly de-

signed MO PRO5800. *Thank you. Please inform pricing.*

LH會提供一個MO BASE3800樣品及一個新設計的MO PRO5800。*謝謝，請告知價格。*

7. Motor Master can accept prototypes from LH and give feedback in return. *Yes, we understand prototypes are meant to evolve.*

Motor Master可以接受LH最原始設計模型並給予回饋。*是的，我們了解原型本來就是要進化。*

8. Motor Master will provide the distance from the rear tire to the kick stand and the pad size of the kick stand. *Yes, as discussed.*

Motor Master會提供後輪到摩托車停車腳架的距離以及腳架圓盤的尺寸。*好，如我們的討論結果。*

TWO CHANGES ABOUT PRODUCTS TO BE MADE. 未來產品的兩個變更

1. The heel of wood packaging should be two inches high.
   木頭包裝的腳架應該為兩吋高。

2. The width of the space for fork lift should be NO LESS than 36 inches, and NO MORE than 44 inches. *Correct.*
   叉車所需的寬度空間應不少於36吋不超過44吋。*正確。*

QUALITY 品質

1. To ensure quality, LH will adopt a camera image matching system for better quality control. *Great news.*
   為確保品質，LH會使用影像比對系統，作更好的品質控管。*好消息。*

2. LH has ISO standards and has formed a quality control system in China. Despite challenges from educating the Chinese workers, to always improve quality to the best is our goal. *Yes, please continue.*

LH在中國有ISO標準，並且已建立一套品質控管系統，即使面對訓練中國工人的挑戰，增進品質永遠是我們的目標。*好，請持續。*

FUTURE GROWTH 未來成長

1. LH and Motor Master will strengthen the ability to reduce the risk from any unpredictable events (e.g., G20). Motor Master will provide half of a year forecast and fulfill at least 70% of sales.

   LH與Motor Master會加強能力以減少任何無法預測事件的風險（例如：G20）。Motor Master會提供半年的預估以及實現至少70%的銷售。

   We will provide a half year ordering forecast, but we are not sure about fulfilling at least 70%. As we are expected to purchase all products on the ordering forecast, our payment terms will change from 30% down payment and 70% at BOL to 100% at BOL. Also, the forecast we provide can lower your raw materials cost. We hope to see, for both of us, some cost savings. Please advise.

   我們會提供半年訂單預估，但我們不能確定至少實現70%。因為我們被期待要購買預估訂單的產品，我們的付款條件要從30%頭期款及70%付款交單，改成100%付款交單。另外，我們提供的預估可以降低你們的原物料成本，我們希望可以見到雙方成本的降低，請告知。

2. LH can provide Motor Master warehouse in Shanghai to consolidate various products to reduce Motor Master sales risks. *Yes, as discussed, good news.*

   LH可以在上海提供Motor Master倉庫用來集貨以降低Motor Master之銷售風險。*是，如我們所討論的，好消息。*

3. In the future, LH and Motor Master can cooperate to sell products

in China or have products go global. *Please send us your plan for this great opportunity!*

將來LH與Motor Master可以合作在中國銷售或全球銷售。*這麼好的機會，請寄給我們你的計畫！*

FOR ROD'S INFORMATION 給羅德的資訊

From your mail, we summarize three key points. 從你的郵件我們整理了三個關鍵。

1. Lead time (on time delivery) 交貨時間（準時到貨）
2. Quality control（品質控制）
3. Price（價格）

We need to get some key information before answering your questions：回答你的問題之前，我們需要得到一些關鍵資訊。

1. About price: what is your sweet spot? *We target at 12% reduction for MO1515 and MO1843. All others at 10% reduction.*
   關於價格：你最理想的價格是什麼？*我們鎖定MO1515跟MO1843降價12%，其他產品10%。*

2. How much quantity will be increased in the future or next year? *At this point, it looks we may be able to increase around 23-28%.*
   將來或明年會有多少增加量？*目前看來我們或許可以增加23-28%。*

3. How long do you wish for your lead time? *With our forecast and your ability to warehouse and consolidate the containers, we wish to ship from your side 10-14 days.*
   你希望交貨到出貨的時間多久？*以我們的預估及你們的倉儲貨櫃集貨能力，我們希望10-14天可以從你們那裡出貨。*

4. What are your questions or concerns about our quality? Or do you have any ideas about our quality? *We hope your products can al-*

ways be improving and remain the highest quality consistently.

你們關於品質的問題與關心是什麼？或者你們有任何關於我們品質的想法嗎？*我們希望你們的產品可以不斷改善，並且一直保持最好的品質。*

5. We hope to increase business with you. How do we cooperate to increase mutual benefits? *If we discuss a project together, we hope to launch the product together with you. Although we had not gotten the first chance to sell MO1157, we have faith to continue to grow together and expand our partnership!*

我們希望與你們增加生意，我們如何合作創造互惠？*如果我們一起討論一個計畫，我們希望與你們一起發行產品。雖然我們沒有獲得第一次銷售MO1157的機會，我們有信心一起持續成長並且擴大我們的夥伴關係。*

客戶來信：重點解讀 Getting the Hidden Messages

1. 「Partnership」出現在頭尾，被強調兩次。
2. 客戶提出之降價幅度很誇張。
3. 價格要求是整批金額或分批出貨金額的30%頭期款？兩者差額很大。
4. 客戶所言「此刻看來」（口氣極不確定）之預計成長率是哪一方面的成長率？
5. 客戶誤導你，讓你以為10-14天就希望你出貨，卻不告訴你要什麼產品？數量多少？如何集貨？

1. The forecast we provide can lower your raw materials cost. We hope to see, for both of us, some cost savings.

   我們提供的預估可以降低原物料的成本，我們希望看到雙方都節省成本。

2. We target at 12% reduction for MO1515 and MO1843. All others at 10% reduction.

   我們的目標是MO1515跟MO1843降價12%，其他產品10%。

3. At this point, it looks we may be able to increase around 23-28%.

   目前看來我們或許可以增加大約23-28%。

4. If we discuss a project together, we hope to launch the product together with you.

   如果我們一起討論一個計畫，我們希望能跟你們一起發行產品。

▶ 技法字詞 Tricky Words and Phrases:

partnership (n.) 夥伴關係

launch together 一起發行

Round 8
第八回合

🗨 新手任務 Your Mission:

你該如何回應？客戶每個項目都回覆了，會議紀錄看來已經密密麻麻，你要如何回應項目？還能照著我們原先的分類嗎？還是必須重新整理分類？客戶的回覆不可行或不合理的部分，你該如何解套？

🗨 試寫Now You Try: 請試寫於下方

（試寫後才翻頁）

依照同意與否加以分類，不可行項目要提出原因及建議。按照happy ending原則（結尾要報喜），安排順序。

▶ 語言祕訣 Language Tips:

1. **不可行**

   will not do

2. **須釐清或討論**

   clarify/discuss more

3. **感謝及可行**

   appreciate/will do

4. **我們需要這兩個答案，才能計算價格變化及交貨期，才能重新報價。**

   We can calculate the change of the price and the lead time only when we have the answers to the two questions.

● 信件範例 Sample Letter:

🐴 我方發信給客戶 Our Email to the Client

Dear Rod,

Thank you for your thorough reply. We have come up with three categories--

1. Will not do:

   Gary's mentioning that the space for fork lift should be no less than 36 inches, and no more than 44 inches. It is impossible for the packaging to withstand long time of transportation.

Suggestions:

(1) Keep the same packaging while marking centralized gravity and the heavy end.

(2) Modify the positions of the heels. Please check the attached file.

(3) Strengthen packaging, but it will add up the cost of packaging.

Please inform your choice.

2. Clarify and discuss:

The price reduction you mentioned is running high hurdles. Please clarify the following points.

(1) The forecast of every product in the next half year.

(2) The payment term: does the 30% down payment refer to the total order or partial order?

We can calculate the change of the price and the lead time only when we have the answers to the two questions. Then, we will requote.

3. Will do:

Will do the rest of the points as you commented above.

Sophie

親愛的羅德：

謝謝你詳細的回覆，我們已分成三類：

1. 不可行：

蓋瑞提到裝卸叉取貨的空間必須在36-44吋之間，但（按此尺寸）包裝將無法承受長久的運輸。

建議：

(1)使用相同包裝，但標示重心與較重的一邊。

(2)修改支架的位置，請見附檔。

(3)加強包裝，但這會增加成本。

請告知你們的選項。

2. 釐清及討論：

你所提的價格太困難，請釐清幾點：

(1)每個產品的半年預期。

(2)付款條件：30%頭期款是指全部訂單或是部分訂單？

我們需要這兩個答案，才能計算價格變化及生產期，才能重新報價。

3. 可行：

其他的項目都可以，如你以上備註。

蘇菲

▶ **關鍵字詞 Key Words and Phrases:**

withstand (v.) 承受

centralized gravity 重心

heavy end 較重的一邊

run high hurdles 跨越高欄

requote (v.) 重新報價

客戶回信 Client's Reply

Dear Sophie,

For our payment terms, I proposed changing from a 30% down payment, 40% at BOL, 30% after a week upon receiving goods confirmation to 100% payment at BOL. We will not have a down payment with a provided forecast. Please confirm.

The attachment is the forecast that we provide. After it is evaluated, the quantity of each item to be consolidated will be provided. With the forecast, we hope the items to be loaded within 2-3 weeks and shipped out.

Thanks again for your wonderful visit to make our partnership grow stronger.

Rod

親愛的蘇菲：

我們的付款條件，我提議從30%頭期款，40%付款交單，30%收貨一週後確認，改爲100%付款交單，我們已經提供預估採購，所以不能付頭期款，請確認。

附件是我們提供的預估採購單，通過評估後，要集貨的每個項目數量會再提供。因爲提供了預估採購量，我們期望能在兩三星期內裝好出貨。

再次感謝你的拜訪，讓我們的夥伴關係更穩固。

羅德

 客戶來信：重點解讀 Getting the Hidden Messages

1. 預估採購量只是先提出，因爲尚未經過評估。
2. 付款改爲100%付款交單，對我們究竟是利是弊？
3. 預估爲整批或分批？

（客戶提出可行不可行之後，同樣以讓人感覺良好之方式結尾。）

1. We will not have a down payment with a provided forecast.

   我們已經提供預估採購，所以不能付頭期款。

2. After it is evaluated, the quantity of each item to be consolidated will be provided.

   通過評估後，再提供要集貨的每個項目數量。

3. With the forecast, we hope the items to be loaded within 2-3 weeks and shipped out.

   因為提供了預估採購量，我們期望能在兩三星期內裝好出貨。

4. Thanks again for your wonderful visit to make our partnership grow stronger.

   再次感謝你的拜訪，讓我們的夥伴關係更穩固。

▶ 技法字詞 Tricky Words and Phrases:

BOL (Bill of Lading), B/L 提單

Round 9
第九回合

● 新手任務 Your Mission:

價格條件改變，對我方究竟是利是弊？你如何回應？

● 試寫Now You Try: 請試寫於下方

（試寫後才翻頁）

教戰守則 Insider Tips

1. 上封信我們問他指的是全部貨款的頭期款或是分批出貨每批的頭期款，他的回覆使我們取得百分百付款及貨物權的優勢，從原本三階段（30% / 40% / 30%）付款改為一階段100%全部付款交單。

2. 我們回覆重點：接受他的提議，不要提到「信任」之相關字，以免招致客戶重新思考翻盤。稍後給他新價格表，以利我方爭取時間，細算成本。

▶ 語言祕訣 Language Tips:

1. 可預見雙方利益

LH is excited to see **the mutual expansion** of both companies.
LH 很樂意見到雙方生意的擴大。

2. 接受付款條件

We confirm to accept your suggestion "payment to 100% payment at Bill of Lading."
我們確認接收你的建議「100% 付款交單」。

3. 將回覆新價格

Please **wait for our new quotations** after my company's meeting. Thanks for your patience.
等本公司內部會議後會盡快回覆給你新的價格表，感謝你的耐心等待！

▶ 關鍵字詞 Key Words and Phrases:

mutual expansion 雙方的擴大

● 信件範例 Sample Letter:

♞ 我方發信給客戶 Our Email to the Client

Dear Rod,

　　Thanks for your reply again. LH is excited to see the mutual expansion of both companies. We confirm to accept your suggestion "payment to 100% payment at Bill of Lading." Please wait for our new quotations after my company's meeting. Thanks for your patience.

　　Sophie

親愛的羅德：

　　謝謝你的回信，LH很樂意見到雙方生意的擴大，我們確認接收你的建議「100% 付款交單」。等本公司內部會議後會盡快回覆給你新的價格表，感謝你的耐心等待！

　　蘇菲

★★★★★★★★★★★★★★目標達成★★★★★★★★★★★★★★
我方成功與對方擴大合作規模，取得價格優勢。

case 06 贏回客戶的訂單
Customer Retention: Getting New Orders

臺灣LH集團 vs 美國GO LIFT公司

客戶與案例背景說明
Background of the Client and the Case

　　美國客戶六十歲猶太裔，過去經營大品牌五金工具類產品，對好品質很有經驗。自行創業二十多年經營手工具及汽車維修工具，員工三十人左右。兒子現爲科學類研究生，可能接班。客戶要求普通工具須具備國際名品的品質，卻只願出路邊攤的價格。

　　客戶與我方生意來往已七八年，但近半年卻沒有任何訂單，頗不尋常，我方猜測可能向其他業者採購。雖然買賣是自由市場，但彼此已有多年生意往來，我方必然具有高CP值產品獲得客戶青睞。如果客戶轉向別人採購，必須適時向對方表示不滿，主動去信了解。

Round 1
第一回合

● 新手任務 Your Mission:

　　你如何發現客戶向他人採購的證據？怎麼表達我方不滿及請對方直說？

（試寫後才翻頁）

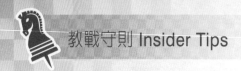

教戰守則 Insider Tips

讓客戶了解我們珍視良好的商業關係，暗示我們已經明白客戶遲未下訂是因為客戶向他人採購了，請客戶對我們產品有意見，應當有話直說。

▶ 語言祕訣 Language Tips:

1. **指出事實**

Since January 2016, **we have not received** your new orders and any comments.

自2016年1月以來我們尚未接到你們的新訂單跟任何消息。

2. **提出猜測**

We then began to wonder whether we had done something which disappointed you?

我們開始懷疑是否曾有任何事令您感到失望？

3. **其他猜測**

Or is it simply that you do not need to order anything at this moment?

或是您只是目前不需要任何訂購？

4. **附上查證後證據**

We found something interesting (please see attachment).

我們發現一件有趣的事（請參閱附件）。

5. **表達不滿**

We sure dislike to see you go across the street because we have had a good business relationship for a lot of years.

我們有許多年的良好商業關係，我們不喜歡您向他人採購。

6. **表達關心與開放溝通**

Whatever the reason, we would like to know how you are doing and **welcome your straightforward comments**.

無論任何理由，我們希望了解您近來如何，並且歡迎您直截了當的意見。

7. **請求告知今年之銷售預計**

Would you **let us know about the sales projections** for GS3000 in the coming year?

是否可請您告知GS3000今年的預計銷售？

▶ 關鍵字詞 Key Words and Phrases:

dislike (v.) 不喜歡

go across the street 向他人採購

straightforward (adj.) 直接的

sales projections 銷售預計

🗨 信件範例 Sample Letter:

♞ 我方發信給客戶 Our Email to the Client

Dear Thomas,

Since January 2016, we have not received your new orders and any comments. We then began to wonder whether we had done something which disappointed you? Or is it simply that you do not need to order anything at this moment?

We found something interesting (please see attachment). We sure dislike to see you go across the street because we have had a good business relationship for a lot of years. Whatever the reason, we would like to know how you are doing and welcome your straightforward comments.

Besides, would you let us know about the sales projections for GS3000 in the coming year?

Best regards,

Sophie

親愛的湯瑪士：

自2016年1月以來我們尚未接到你們的新訂單跟任何消息，我們開始懷疑是否曾有任何事令您感到失望？或是您只是目前不需要任何訂購？

我們發現一件有趣的事（請參閱附件）。我們有許多年的良好商業關係，我們不喜歡您向他人採購。無論任何理由，我們希望了解您近來如何，並且歡迎您直截了當的意見。

此外，是否可請您告知GS3000今年的預計銷售？

誠摯祝福，

蘇菲

 內行必知 Insider Must-Know

如何查證客戶是否向競爭對手採購？

答案就在你是否內行，知道可從查詢海關交易資料中，發現線索。當然還有網路、論壇或其他銷售管道可以發現線索。

♟ 客戶回信 Client's Reply

http://...

http://...

http://...

http://...

♞ 客戶來信：重點解讀 Getting the Hidden Messages

客戶回覆四個產品的網路連結，無隻字片語，令人摸不著頭緒，你只能猜測他的用意。其中兩個產品向我方購買，另兩個產品不是。

Round 2
第二回合

● 新手任務 Your Mission:

客戶只回連結，你該怎麼回信？

● 試寫Now You Try: 請試寫於下方

（試寫後才翻頁）

教戰守則 Insider Tips

　　我們推測客戶可能請其他廠商山寨我公司的產品，以取得低價購入牟利。我們一方面要提出專利證明並且向他請求介紹美國律師的方式嚇阻他，另一方面也要他有話直說，然後以感謝對方意見結尾。

▶ **語言祕訣 Language Tips:**

1. 表達猜測

We think you **have probably misunderstood us**.
我們猜測您應當是誤會了。

2. 解釋網頁之被仿冒產品

The other two products on the webpages are **pirated goods of my company's products**.
另外兩個網頁上的兩項產品是仿冒本公司的產品。

3. 告知已提出法律訴訟

We have taken legal action against the copycats.
我們已經對他們採取法律行動。

4. 請求介紹美國律師（以嚇阻客戶想在中國山寨我產品）

Could you please kindly **introduce an American attorney** in this field to us?
您可以介紹美國這方面的律師給我們嗎？

5. 提出專利證據（附件）

Please refer to the attachment that shows **our patent in the US**.
附件是我們在美國的專利讓您參考。

6. **表示重視客戶**

    You are a **valued customer**.

    您是本公司很重要的客戶。

7. **請求有意見直說**

    If there is anything about our products and services that have
    ever disappointed you, please **give us straightforward com-
    ments**.

    若我們有讓您失望的地方，請直接跟我們說。

8. **感謝支持**

    We appreciate your valuable opinions and your long-term
    support.

    我們很珍惜您寶貴的意見，並感謝您長期的支持！

▶ 關鍵字詞 Key Words and Phrases:

misunderstand (v.) 誤會

pirated goods 山寨品

take legal action 採取法律行動

copycats (n.) 山寨商

attorney (n.) 律師

patent (n.) 專利

straightforward (adj.) 直截了當的

🐴 我方發信給客戶 Our Email to the Client

Dear Thomas,

We think you have probably misunderstood us. The following two brands belong to the same company, while the other two products on the webpages are pirated goods of my company's products. We have taken legal action against the copycats. Could you please kindly introduce an American attorney in this field to us? Please refer to the attachment that shows our patent in the US.

You are a valued customer. If there is anything about our products and services that have ever disappointed you, please give us straightforward comments. We appreciate your valuable opinions and your long-term support.

Best regards,

Sophie

親愛的湯瑪士：

我們猜測您應當是誤會了，下列兩個品牌屬於同一公司，另外兩個網頁不是本公司的產品，而是仿冒本公司的產品，我們已經對他們採取法律行動。您可以介紹美國這方面的律師給我們嗎？附件是我們在美國的專利讓您參考。

您是本公司很重要的客戶，若我們有讓您失望的地方，請直接跟我們說。我們很珍惜您寶貴的意見，並感謝您長期的支持！

誠摯祝福，

蘇菲

客戶回信 Client's Reply

Sophie,

Could you please have Frank call me asap?

Thomas

蘇菲：

請法蘭克盡快打電話給我。

湯瑪士

客戶來信：重點解讀 Getting the Hidden Messages

　　客戶只有一句話，要跟你的主管對談。美國客戶跟我們講電話有英語優勢，我們處下風，容易被占便宜。再者，電話內容可能講不清楚又沒任何紀錄，有爭議時容易各說各話，變成羅生門。客戶會有什麼要求？要如何準備？如何應對？

Round 3
第三回合

● 新手任務 Your Mission:
寫下你的預測與準備。

● 試寫Now You Try: 請試寫於下方

（試寫後才翻頁）

教戰守則 Insider Tips

明知客戶可藉著講電話取得優勢，但他是客戶，我們不得不打，最好準備錄音，並一定要做通話紀錄，事後寄給客戶確認內容。記得聽不懂要問，客戶提到的點要確認他真正的意思，但不可輕易同意或承諾，而是說你記下他的意見，將以信件回覆。

我方品質受客戶肯定，預期客戶提出關鍵的質疑及要求在於：

1. 價格：某對手賣得好，是因為我方供貨價錢較低？
2. 交貨時間：為何我方供貨給對手的交貨時間較短？客戶要求縮短交貨時間。

▶ 語言祕訣 Language Tips:

1. 解釋客戶價格質疑

They sell well because they sell lots of goods.
他們賣得好是因為他們賣很多產品。

2. 反轉情勢

Do you want to sell a variety of products?
你想多賣些產品嗎？

3. 回答客戶交貨時間的要求

We will check about time and get back to you.
我們會查看時間（不能應允）再回覆。

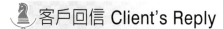
客戶回信 Client's Reply

Hi, Sophie,

How are you? How long will it take to get another container of GS3000 ready for shipment? The next shipment is on Aug. 1, right?

Thomas

嗨，蘇菲：

你好嗎？GS3000要多久才能準備好？下次出貨是8月1日，對嗎？

湯瑪士

客戶來信：重點解讀 Getting the Hidden Messages

因為我們有專利，而且對客戶解釋其對手賣得好的原因在於種類多，讓零售客人選擇多。這兩點就讓客戶回頭，產生動力，現在客戶急著要貨了！

Round 4
第四回合

新手任務 Your Mission:

客戶催下訂的交貨時間，你該怎麼回？先寫寫看。

試寫Now You Try: 請試寫於下方

（試寫後才翻頁）

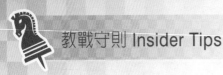

你回答的交貨時間，必須取得恐怖平衡。也就是說，我們要讓客戶知道實力，讓客戶學到這次經驗，不再跟別家廠商購買，或甚至要其他廠商山寨我們的產品。

▶ 語言祕訣 Language Tips:

1. 告知資訊

Within 10 days, the container **will be ready**. The vessel booking schedule will soon be sent to you once confirmed.

十天內貨櫃會準備好，預訂的船班一旦確定了，就會通知你。

2. 告知新貨出貨期

A new container **can be ready around Oct. 20** due to the coming of G20.

因為G20的緣故，新的貨櫃要10月20日才能準備好。

3. 解釋原因

Because the China government demands cleaning up air pollution during the build-up and the summit of G20 in Sep., our factory will be forced to shut down for 12 days.

因為中國政府要求在九月G20建造及高峰會期間淨化空汙，所以我們的工廠要被迫關閉十二天。

▶ 關鍵字詞 Key Words and Phrases:

demand (v.) 要求

summit (n.) 高峰會

force (v.) 強迫

shut down 關閉

📣 信件範例 Sample Letter:

♟ 我方發信 Our Reply

Dear Thomas,

Within 10 days, the container will be ready. The vessel booking schedule will soon be sent to you once confirmed.

A new container can be ready around Oct. 20 due to the coming of G20. Because the China government demands cleaning up air pollution during the build-up and the summit in Sep., our factory will be forced to shut down for 12 days, like all other factories, businesses, schools, and traffic systems of the city.

Best,

Sophie

親愛的湯瑪士：

十天內貨櫃會準備好，預訂的船班一旦確定了，就會通知你。

因為G20的緣故，新的貨櫃要10月20日才能準備好。因為中國政府要求在九月G20建造及高峰會期間淨化空汙，所以我們的工廠（跟城市內的其他工廠、商店、學校、交通系統一樣），要被迫關閉十二天。

誠摯祝福，

蘇菲

客戶回信 Client's Reply

Sophie,

　　Can you make it faster than Oct. 20? It used to take a month to make and another month to ship, but now it is taking more than three months to wait. It is taking too long. I want the first container to arrive for inspection before I can place another order.

　　Thomas

蘇菲：

　　你可以趕在10月20日前嗎？通常要一個月來做跟另一個月來運送，現在要等三個月，實在太久了，我要第一個貨櫃抵達及驗過貨，才能下另一個訂單。

　　湯瑪士

客戶來信：重點解讀 Getting the Hidden Messages

　　我們可以研判客戶可能已經取消前面跟他人購買的訂單，所以急著催促我們的貨物。礙於2016年G20在中國杭州舉辦，而產生許多不可抗力的管制，客人雖不耐久候也沒辦法（儘管如此，我們仍須設法先滿足他一批貨的要求）。

　　先前我們問他的今年預估採購量，客戶的回答是「無法預估」，因爲他想收到一批貨檢驗後，再下另一訂單。

Round 5
第五回合

● 新手任務 Your Mission:
　客戶催下訂的交貨時間，你怎麼回？先寫寫看。

● 試寫Now You Try: 請試寫於下方

（試寫後才翻頁）

教戰守則 Insider Tips

面對不可抗力能做的事有限，只有下次提早下訂單才能消除不確定因素。

▶ **語言祕訣 Language Tips:**

1. **告知現況**

   Right now, our production line is all full and cannot make it any time earlier than Oct. 20.

   現在我們的生產線全滿，新的貨櫃無法早於10月20日前完成。

2. **表達歉意**

   We are sorry about the unexpected closure for G20.

   因為G20造成未預期的工廠關閉我們很抱歉。

3. **提醒（我們給他的新遊戲規則）**

   Please place your next order in advance.

   請你新的訂單要提早下。

▶ **關鍵字詞 Key Words and Phrases:**

full (adj.) 充滿的

unexpected closure 無預期關閉

in advance 事先，提早

🐴 我方發信 Our Reply

Dear Thomas,

Right now, our production line is all full and cannot make it any time earlier than Oct. 20. We are sorry about the unexpected closure for G20. Please place your next order in advance.

Best,

Sophie

親愛的湯瑪士：

現在我們的生產線全滿，新的貨櫃無法早於10月20日前完成。因為G20造成未預期的工廠關閉我們很抱歉，請你新的訂單要提早下。

誠摯祝福，

蘇菲

🐎 客戶回信 Client's Reply

Dear Sophie,

Could you have Frank call me asap about more orders? I'm traveling now.

Thanks.

Thomas

親愛的蘇菲：

請法蘭克盡快打電話給我談更多的訂單，我現在旅行中。

謝謝。

湯瑪士

客戶來信：重點解讀 Getting the Hidden Messages

　　客人無貨可賣，所以去旅行了嗎？可能並非如此，而是他想要更早弄到更多的貨，並且急了。季節的轉變可能讓訂貨變得風險，客戶要訂貨卻不來信用白紙黑字寫（所以說他在旅行），而是要跟主管講電話談條件，你知道他故技重施，又要打「電話牌」了。（見附錄二）

Round 6
第六回合

與客戶在美國辦公室會面（會議紀錄）
Meeting the Client in His US Office (Minutes)

　　（請見個案五教戰守則：與國外客戶開會之準備）
　　佛心的主管，已幫你把開完會之紀錄以中文條列，如下：

親愛的湯瑪士：

　　法蘭克很高興與你會面，希望我們能有更好的未來。

　　2016年7月20日的會議紀錄如下：

1. 為了加快出貨速度，請Go Lift提供半年或一年的預測訂單。
2. 為使預測與生產量調和穩定，出貨量需達到預測量之70%。
3. LH須更新網頁及目錄，在未全面完成更新之前，若有新產品，要及時更新給Go Lift；相對地，Go Lift會優先向LH提出產品詢價或任何想法的討論。

4. 爲了因應市場的變化，LH會提供併櫃服務，並以最優化的裝貨量來出貨。

5. Go Lift 願意各購買一臺LH的高壓清洗機及空氣壓縮機，LH會附上機車攜帶架，供Go Lift做性能測試。

6. Go Lift請LH試著修改GS5105的側邊板從2片變爲4片。

7. 若遇緊急需求時，以工廠現有產品來出貨。

8. GS2823一個CMB的數量是100臺，若你同意這個數量，我將會修改訂單後，回傳給你確認。

以上紀錄，如有遺漏未登錄者，請補充，謝謝！

蘇菲

● 新手任務 Your Mission:

你必須將主管整理出來的會議紀錄寫成英文，請試作。

● 試寫Now You Try: 請試寫於下方

（試寫後才翻頁）

● 範例：會議紀錄初稿Sample: Meeting Minutes Draft

GO LIFT and LH Meeting Minutes
07/20/2016 9:00-12:00 a.m.
Location: Go Lift Office
Participants: Go Lift (Thomas Wolf, Sandy Jones)
LH (Frank Lin, Sophie Wong)

Dear Thomas,

Frank had a wonderful meeting with you. We hope to have a better future with you together. Please see the meeting minutes that I summarize from the meeting with Frank on 07.20.2016.

1. To ensure on-time shipment, Go Lift will provide a half year or a year forecast in advance.

2. To ensure the stability between forecast and production, 70% of the forecast order should be executed.

3. LH's websites and catalogs need to be updated. Before the whole-scale update is completed, LH will update any new products for Go Lift. In return, Go Lift will give LH the priority to answer any inquiries or discuss any new ideas.

4. To adjust for market, LH will consolidate products to the best possible loading capacity for Go Lift.

5. Go Lift will purchase one pressure washer and one air compressor, while LH will provide a scooter carrier for Go Lift to test its performance.

6. LH will try to modify GS5105 side extension for Go Lift from two pieces to four pieces.

7. The shipment will deliver stock products when there is an emer-

gent demand.

8. Each CBM can hold 100 GS2823. If Go Lift agrees with this number, LH will modify the order for Go Lift to confirm.

Could you please add any comments if there is missing information?

Best regards,

Sophie

▶ 語言祕訣 Language Tips:

原本按照會議進行的順序，必須按照邏輯歸納順序。

新順序為：17248653（括弧內為舊順序）

● 會議紀錄（順序歸納）

1. (1) 為了加快出貨速度，請Go Lift提供半年或一年的預測訂單。

   To ensure on-time shipment, Go Lift will provide a half year or a year forecast in advance.

2. (7) 若遇緊急需求時，以現貨來出貨。

   The shipment will deliver stock products when there is an emergent demand.

3. (2) 為使預測與生產量調和穩定，出貨量需達到預測量之70%。

   To ensure the stability between forecast and production, 70% of the forecast order should be executed.

4. (4) 為因應市場變化，LH會為Go Lift以最優化的裝貨量集貨。

   To adjust for market, LH will consolidate products to the best possible loading capacity for Go Lift.

5. (8) GS2823一個CMB的數量是100臺，若Go Lift同意這個數量，LH將會修改訂單後，回傳給GO Lift確認。

   Each CBM can hold 100 GS2823. If Go Lift agrees with this

number, LH will modify the order for Go Lift to confirm.

6. (6) Go Lift請LH試著修改GS5105的側邊板，從2片變為4片。

   LH will try to modify GS5105 side extension for Go Lift from two pieces to four pieces.

7. (5) Go Lift 願意各購買一臺LH的高壓清洗機及空氣壓縮機，LH會附上機車攜帶架，供Go Lift做性能測試。

   Go Lift will purchase one pressure washer and one air compressor, while LH will provide a scooter carrier for Go Lift to test its performance.

8. (3) LH須更新網頁及目錄，在未全面完成更新之前，若有新產品，要及時更新給Go Lift；相對地，Go Lift會優先向LH提出產品詢價或任何想法的討論。

   LH's websites and catalogs need to be updated. Before the whole-scale update is completed, LH will update any new products for Go Lift. In return, Go Lift will give LH the priority to answer any inquiries and discuss any new ideas.

▶ 關鍵字詞 Key Words and Phrases:

forecast (v.) 預測

stock (n.) 存貨

emergent demand 緊急需求

stability (n.) 穩定性

adjust (v.) 因應，調整

consolidate (v.) 集貨

loading capacity 裝載量

update (v.) 更新

範例：會議紀錄Sample: Meeting Minutes

GO LIFT AND LH MEETING MINUTES

07/20/2016 9:00-12:00 a.m.

Location: Go Lift Office

Participants: Go Lift (Thomas Wolf, Sandy Jones)

LH (Frank Lin, Sophie Wong)

Dear Thomas,

Frank had a wonderful meeting with you. We hope to have a better future with you together. Please see the meeting minutes that I summarize from the meeting with Frank on 07.20.2016.

1. To ensure on-time shipment, Go Lift will provide a half year or a year forecast in advance.

2. The shipment will deliver stock products when there is an emergent demand.

3. To ensure the stability between forecast and production, 70% of the forecast order should be executed.

4. To adjust for market, LH will consolidate products to the best possible loading capacity for Go Lift.

5. Each CBM can hold 100 GS2823. If Go Lift agrees with this number, LH will modify the order for Go Lift to confirm.

6. LH will try to modify GS5105 side extension for Go Lift from two pieces to four pieces.

7. Go Lift will purchase one pressure washer and one air compressor, while LH will provide a scooter carrier for Go Lift to test its performance.

8. LH's websites and catalogs need to be updated. Before the whole-scale update is completed, LH will update any new products for Go Lift. In return, Go Lift will give LH the priority to answer any inquiries or discuss any new ideas.

Could you please add any comments if there is missing information?

Best regards,

Sophie

▶ 為何LEAD TIME（交貨時間）是個問題？

2008年金融危機之前的榮景期，客戶會提供預估採購量，但2008年後，客戶無把握能否如期銷售，不願承擔財務風險，只想提供一次的短期採購。也就是說，現在的客戶既不願提供預估的半年或一年採購量，卻又要求下單短時間就要交貨，但訂單及交貨時間的解決之道無他，還是在於雙方須能先行預測。

★★★★★★★★★★★★★★目標達成★★★★★★★★★★★★★★
我方成功贏回客戶，並要求對方先提供採購量，取得部分之主控優勢。

case 07 進口商以零售商要求為由將成本轉嫁供應商
Client Passing Retailer's Cost onto the Supplier

臺灣LH集團 VS 美國PRIME MOTOR公司

客戶與案例背景說明
Background of the Client and the Case

　　臺灣移民美國第二代夫婦（家族已三代從事本行生意），皆三十歲左右，先生Peter為總經理（General Manager, GM），太太Elaine 為辦公室總管（Chief of Office, COO）兩人皆在十歲前自臺灣移民美國，英文成為母語，懂中文但會讀不會寫，懂中國文化，具商業頭腦，有長輩當參謀，企業規模為有兩百多位員工之進口商公司及工廠，近年已成美國中部之越野工具及農機具進口大盤商之一。在中國有十多人之專門驗貨員，雖說驗貨一切按照規章標準來，但驗貨員怕被公司認為不盡責，一定會挑產品或包裝毛病，我方為供應商，就會面臨罰則（罰金）及退貨。

　　雙方生意往來數年，與我方電話或會議溝通雖偶有中文交談，但彼此書面接洽皆以英文溝通，因此對方占語言優勢。我方派員與客戶談可行性罰則，但對方先生只願跟我方主管談，太太也要跟我方主管談折讓，也就是說夫婦兩人同時開闢戰場，兩人聯手使我方主管一人分身乏術，疲於應付！我方主管必須小心應對，策略為選擇關閉一戰場。

　　我方之另一隱憂為對方資本雄厚，極可能會請第三地廠商仿冒我方擁有專利，但不久後專利即將到期之產品，以大量進口低價搶走美國市場。客戶之所以可能這麼做是因為法律可以起訴製造仿冒品之工廠，但無法追溯到進口商。我方與客戶往來必須考慮如何持續保有商機，並防杜危機。

🐚客戶來信（會議紀錄）Letter (Meeting Minutes) from the Client

我方與對方商務拜訪後，當天晚上即收到客戶所做之會議紀錄如下：

Dear Frank,

Thank you for the wonderful visit today. After our meeting, our EVP Kevin and I summed up a few points together. First, I brought up to Kevin that we have requested requoting of our current products. We have also expected to receive some samples for possible purchases in the future. He likes both ideas and has mentioned our intense competition with the rivals. To keep our business, Kevin asks if we can have your rebate support for our customer program. Would you agree to support us with 3% in rebate on the sales starting from 2017? We appreciate your services and sincerely hope that you'd agree to help us out in the current business situations.

We look forward to your reply, and thanks very much again for your visit.

Best,

Elaine

親愛的法蘭克：

謝謝你今天的美好拜訪，在我們的會議之後，本公司的執行副總凱文跟我一起彙整會議重點。首先，我向凱文提到要求現有產品的重新報價。我們也期待收到一些樣品，將來可能購買。凱文覺得這些想

法很好，也提到我們與對手的強力競爭。為了保持生意，凱文提到是否可以請你支持我們的顧客折讓方案，你是否能同意自2017年起折讓售價的3%？我們很感謝你的服務，並且誠心希望你能同意在現在的景氣情況下幫助我們。

我們期盼你的回音，再次感謝你的來訪。

誠摯祝福，

依蓮

● 會議紀錄分析 Analyzing the Minutes/Reply:

客戶馬上發信謝謝我方去拜訪，並且用來當作會議紀錄（meeting minutes）。如果當天我方有隨行人擔任紀錄，在雙方都有紀錄的情形下，誰先發出會議紀錄，誰就擁有話語權。遺憾的是此次拜訪我方僅主管一人赴會，沒有隨行之紀錄人員，我方因失去製作會議紀錄之話語權而處於劣勢（對比個案五），必須非常謹慎檢閱對方所作之紀錄，發現任何不利我方情勢之記載，要努力扳回劣勢。

我方主管與客戶Peter主談，Elaine記錄，但Elaine顯然才是操盤人。此次會議紀錄客戶使用幾招策略，非常不利我方，你看的出來嗎？請先試寫。

● 試寫Now You Try: 請試寫於下方

（試寫後才翻頁）

客戶來信：重點解讀 Getting the Hidden Messages

1. 借刀殺人：Kevin是執行副總，但當天並未參與會議（我方主管知道Kevin）。Elaine將Kevin提到檯面，是預備動作，先以他的名義要求降價，將來還會打出其他變化球。

2. 母語為英語的Peter及Elaine，以後如以Kevin名義投變化球或由Kevin寫信，我們用英語談生意恐會處於劣勢。

3. 客戶製造可能表象，給予我方甜頭（some samples for possible purchases）。

4. 我方專利到期前，怕我方不供貨，卻又要求降價（starting from 2017）。

5. 客戶打了詭字牌（附錄二），用了一個貿易往來不常用的字「rebate」，這字有「退回貨款」的意思，我們為什麼要退回貨款？用這字顯然有設陷阱的用意。要求rebate，也就是要轉嫁他們零售給顧客的成本給我方。

6. 客戶了解我們手上握有中國專利，而且快到期了，一來怕我們不出貨或延遲出貨給他們，二來也知道2017年是專利的最後一年，所以才會用2017年起退3%給他們。

▶ 語言陷阱 Language Traps:

1. After our meeting, our EVP Kevin and I summed up a few points together.
   在我們的會議之後，本公司的執行副總Kevin跟我一起彙整會議重點。

2. First, I brought up to Kevin that we have requested requoting of our current products.
   首先，我向Kevin提到要求現有產品的重新報價。

3. We have also expected to receive some samples for possible purchases in the future.

我們也期待收到一些樣品，將來可能購買。

4. To keep our business, Kevin asks if we can have your rebate support for our customer program.

為了保持生意，Kevin提到是否可以請你支持我們的顧客折讓方案。

5. Would you agree to support us with 3% in rebate on the sales starting from 2017?

你是否能同意自2017年起折讓售價的3%？

6. We appreciate your services and sincerely hope that you'd agree to help us out in the current business situations.

我們很感謝你的服務，並且誠心希望你能同意在現在的景氣情況下幫助我們。

▶ 技法字詞 Tricky Words and Phrases:

EVP (executive vice president) 執行副總

possible purchases 可能購買

intense competition 強力競爭

rival (n.) 對手

rebate (n.) 折讓

🗨 新手任務 Your Mission:

沒想到在主管看似成功拜訪後，當天晚上就收到充滿詭雷的會議紀錄，根本沒有參與會議的對方執行副總被牽扯進來，客戶還連投給我們幾個變化球。因為沒有隨行人員做紀錄，我們真的被將了一軍！在會議結束後莫名衍生出無關會議的轉嫁成本問題。

客戶可謂笑談間用兵，我們該如何解脫困境？

● 試寫Now You Try: 請試寫於下方

想想看，Elaine寫這個會議紀錄的用意何在？

1. Elaine想拉高層級讓Kevin直接對付我方業務經理（Kevin雖是執行副總，但也是員工，可以直截了當地指東道西）。

2. Elaine用rebate警告我方，競爭對手（亦向我方採購）搶了他們的生意，要我方降價或補償他們的損失。

3. 雖然在會議上，我方主管表明價格可由業務Jessie做主，但Elaine仍然直接把信傳給主管Frank。

你覺得我方主管會親自回信給Elaine或是指派誰來回信？回信給誰？副本給誰？內容怎麼回？關於rebate這個陷阱字，你來回信的話，要如何拆招？

_____

_____

_____

_____

_____

_____

_____

_____

_____

_____

（試寫後才翻頁）

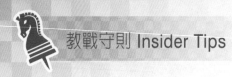

雙方人員往來按權力運作之職級可分上、中、下駒如下：

權力／職級		我方	客戶
上	主管	Frank	Elaine跟Peter
中	業務	Jessie	EVP Kevin
下	業務助理	Nina	Ron

　　Peter、Elaine、Kevin三人看似有某種權力運作，但三人又各自扮演上、中、下駒。要拆解Elaine用中駒Kevin對我們的上駒主管的招術，我們必須在回信時使用中駒對中駒，也就是由業務Jessie寫給EVP Kevin，並善用email副本功能，副本給Elaine。

　　另外，你知道rebate是零售商與消費者之間的折讓，進出口業者並不使用。儘管如此，你必須在禮貌上請Elaine解釋此字定義。所有的文字都必須考慮周到，一來要顧到客戶讀信的感受，二來要給自己保留轉圜空間，不要挖洞給自己跳。

▶ 語言祕訣 Language Tips:

1. **表達感謝與敬佩**

We **appreciate** your support and understanding of our business and **greatly admire** your perseverance and commitment as the third generation in the honorable family.

感謝貴公司過去這些年的支持與理解，我們非常敬佩你們作為家族第三代承擔起承先啟後的重擔。

2. 彼此溝通解決問題

We also believe that we will **continue to communicate**, encourage each other, and solve problems together.

相信我們兩家公司會持續溝通順暢，遇到問題時，可以互相鼓勵及共同解決問題。

3. 請求理解

We would like to apologize for any of our linguistic glitches before that came **from good intentions**.

我們很抱歉，如果有任何因為求好心切而造成的言語不周。

4. 解釋用字

Before answering your request about lowering the price from 2017, **could you please explain** the word "rebate" for its rare use in our exporting business writing?

在回答你的要求2017年降價前，想請你解釋「rebate」這個字，因為在我們出口業是很少用到的字。

5. 為將來留伏筆

LH is willing to cooperate to expand your business. **If there are no accidents, we may be able to** meet your request about lowering 3% in price from 2017.

LH非常願意配合貴公司的業務擴大發展，若沒有任何意外，我們願意在2017年開始，盡可能的滿足你降價3%的要求。

▶ 關鍵字詞 Key Words and Phrases:

honorable (adj.) 可敬的，正直的

glitches (n.) 瑕疵，失靈

good intentions 好意

rare use 鮮少使用

accidents (n.) 意外

meet your request 達成你的要求

● 信件範例 Sample Letter:

我方發信給客戶 Our Email to the Client

Dear Elaine and Peter,

How are you? Frank has mentioned to me your wonderful meeting. We appreciate your support and understanding of our business and greatly admire your perseverance and commitment as the third generation in the honorable family. We also believe that we will continue to communicate, encourage each other, and solve problems together. Meanwhile, we would like to apologize for any of our linguistic glitches before that came from good intentions.

Before answering your request about lowering the price from 2017, could you please explain the word "rebate"for its rare use in our exporting business? LH is willing to cooperate to expand your business. If there are no accidents, we may be able to meet your request about lowering 3% in price from 2017.

Best regards,

Jessie

親愛的依蓮與彼得：

您好！法蘭克有跟我提起你們愉快的會面，感謝貴公司過去這

些年的支持與理解，我們非常敬佩你們作為家族第三代承擔起承先啓後的重擔。也相信我們兩家公司會持續溝通順暢，遇到問題時，可以互相鼓勵及共同解決問題。如果有任何因為求好心切而造成的言語不周，我們很抱歉。

在回答你的要求2017年降價前，想請你解釋「rebate」這個字，因為在我們出口業是很少用到的字。LH非常願意配合貴公司的業務擴大發展，若沒有任何意外，我們願意在2017年開始，盡可能的滿足你降價3%的要求。

誠摯祝福，

潔西

註：1.回覆信件未副本給Kevin（EVP）的原因在於不要增加無謂之戰場。Kevin沒參加會議，雖然被Elaine在紀錄裡拉進來，我方就要把他拉出去。

2.「如果有任何因為求好心切而造成的言語不周，我們很抱歉。」添加此句消弭我方業務與對方驗貨員曾有過的口舌之爭。如案例背景所言，對方驗貨員怕被公司認為不盡責，而挑產品或包裝的毛病，我方業務難免不耐煩，因客戶只聽驗貨員一面之詞，我方就面臨採購商的罰則（罰金）及退貨。

Round 2
第二回合

客戶回信 Client's Reply

Frank,

We have provided our customer Max Plus a planogram that sells all products from LH. The planogram offers Max Plus 10% rebate each season to keep the business. For this reason, we are asking for 3% deduction of the goods we purchase from you starting from 2017. Year to date, we have purchased around $170,000, and 3% rebate is about $5,100. If you agree to help us out, our accountant department will issue a Debit Memo with the exact amount of the 3% rebate to be deducted against payment. Please advise.

Also, would you please send us 2017 pricing update for our PO preparation?

Thanks and best regards,

Elaine

法蘭克：

我們提供給（零售商）客戶Max Plus一個貨價圖，銷售所有來自LH的產品。為了保有生意，這個貨價圖我們提供給Max Plus每季10%的折讓，因此我們請求2017年起我們向你們購買的產品減價3%。今年至今，我們已經向你們買了大約$170,000的貨品，3%大約是$5,100。如果你同意幫忙，我們的會計部門會發出借記備註文件，載明3%的確實金額，從付款中扣除，請指示。

另外，可否寄來2017年貨品的價格更新，讓我們準備訂單？

謝謝與誠摯祝福，

依蓮

 客戶來信：重點解讀 Getting the Hidden Messages

注意到了嗎？Elaine回信層級拉高，跳過業務Jessie（中駒），直接寫給主管Frank（上駒）！

客戶重提他們跟零售業之間的生意，因為銷售架上賣的全是我們的產品，客戶要保有上架生意而提供零售商折讓，藉此要求我們吸收他們的成本，減價3%。客戶接著提出今年的訂貨量以及要扣減之金額，並且再度暗示如果我們同意減價的話，就可以準備接訂單了。

▶ 語言陷阱 Language Traps:

1. We have provided our customer Max Plus a planogram that sells all products from LH.

   我們提供給（零售商）客戶Max Plus一個貨價圖，銷售所有來自LH的產品。

2. The planogram offers Max Plus 10% rebate each season to keep the business.

   為了保有生意，這個貨價圖我們提供給Max Plus每季10%的折讓。

3. For this reason, we are asking for 3% deduction of the goods we purchase from you starting from 2017.

   因此我們請求2017年起我們向你們購買的產品減價3%。

4. Year to date, we have purchased around $170,000, and 3% rebate is about $5,100.

   今年至今，我們已經向你們買了大約$170,000的貨品，3%大約是$5,100。

5. If you agree to help us out, our accountant department will issue a Debit Memo with the exact amount of the 3% rebate to be deducted against payment. Please advise.

   如果你同意幫忙，我們的會計部門會發出借記備註文件，載明3%的確實金額，從付款中扣除，請指示。

6. Would you please send us 2017 pricing update for our PO prep-

aration?

可否寄來2017年貨品的價格更新，讓我們準備訂單？

▶ 技法字詞 Tricky Words and Phrases:

planogram (n.) 貨價圖

to keep the business 為了保有生意

year to date 今年至今

debit memo 借記備註

deduct (v.) 扣除

● 新手任務 Your Mission:

　　公司能同意降價嗎？顧客轉嫁他們跟顧客之間的成本給我們，如果我們同意降價，以後可能回不去了，怎麼辦呢？

● 試寫Now You Try: 請試寫於下方

_____

_____

_____

_____

_____

_____

_____

_____

（試寫後才翻頁）

　　這種要求降價的信不要急著回應，免得被誤會有較大利潤空間可降價，議題暫時擱置（三四天或一週），若還有其他事項要討論，先挑有利我方或有利於雙方的議題。我方繼續要業務Jessie（中駒）回信給Elaine（上駒），我方主管Frank不出面。

　　關於價錢，我方不能輕易同意rebate，無論rebate（折讓）或refund（退貨／退款）這些字，對我們都極為不利：除了喪失利潤，還可能隱含我們的貨品有問題，可謂賠了夫人又折兵。如果情勢所逼，逃不掉的話，要挑一個有利於我方的同義字，例如：donate（捐獻）。雖然犧牲一些金錢，你能體會到雙方的關係瞬間改變嗎？當我們說「捐獻」，客戶還好意思接受嗎？

　　買賣雙方每天都有許多挑戰要面對，生意要持續下去必須通權達變，想辦法化解困難，也就是俗話說的「你有你的張良計，我有我的過牆梯。」除非能生產全世界無可取代的產品，價格才能操之在我。如果有利潤空間，也為了將來和諧（驗貨），可給予少許新訂單「提前」降價空間。如此，明年就有籌碼不降價。記住在願意答應降價的同時，是否有但書要考慮清楚。顧客是否會得寸進尺，拿到較低的新價錢就回頭跟你砍現在手上還未出貨的單子？

▶ 語言祕訣 Language Tips:

1. 強調行業不熟悉的用字

Again, the word "rebate" is **not a familiar term** in our exporting business.

「rebate」這個字在出口業依然不是我們所熟悉的字彙。

2. **負擔超乎預期**

We all have our challenges to face every day and **have not expected** the cost to cover your customers.

大家都有自己的挑戰需要面對，本公司沒有預期到要負擔貴公司顧客的成本。

3. **如無意外願意讓步**

We are willing to lower 1% of price in advance starting from Oct. 1, 2016 (see attachment for new quotations) **if there are no accidents**.

如無任何意外，本公司願意從2016年10月1日起，新的訂單就提前降價1%（請參考附檔新的報價單）。

4. **生效條件**

Please also understand **only after** all items of the previous orders are shipped out by Sep. 30, 2016 **can we start to** lower the 1% of price.

請了解只有在2016年9月30日前，所有先前的訂單全數出貨完畢，我們才能開始降低價格1%。

● 信件範例 Sample Letter:

🐴 我方發信給客戶 Our Email to the Client

Dear Elaine and Peter,

Thanks for explaining the word "rebate." Again, it is not a familiar term in our exporting business.

We all have our challenges to face every day and have not expected the cost to cover your customers. However, to thank your continuing business over the years and to encourage each other, <u>we are willing</u> <u>to lower 1% of price in advance starting from Oct. 1, 2016 (see attachment for new quotations) if there are no accidents. Please also understand only after all items of the previous order PO#2485 are shipped out by Sep. 30, 2016 can we start to lower the 1% of price.</u>

LH wholeheartedly welcomes Peter's new factory visit in China on Aug. 25. We are sorry to inform you that Frank is not available that day due to other business. Our China operator, Rae, will be meeting Peter for the process of auto tools production.

Best regards,

Jessie

親愛的依蓮與彼得：

謝謝你解釋「rebate」的定義，但是「rebate」這個字在出口業依然不是我們所熟悉的字彙。

大家都有自己的挑戰需要面對，本公司沒有預期到要負擔貴公司顧客的成本。但為了表示本公司感激貴公司一直以來的支持，<u>如無任何意外，本公司願意從2016年10月1日起，新的訂單就提前降價1%（請參考附檔新的報價單）。請了解只有在2016年9月30日前，所有先前的訂單全數出貨完畢，我們才能開始降低價格1%。</u>

LH歡迎彼得8月25日拜訪中國的新廠，到時會由瑞伊全程陪同彼得了解汽車工具的製作過程，法蘭克因有其他行程，當日將無法陪同，在此先行致歉。

誠摯祝福，

潔西

familiar (adj.) 熟悉的

expect (v.) 預料

challenge (n.) 挑戰

encourage (v.) 鼓勵

Round 3
第三回合

 客戶來信 Letter from the Client

Dear Jessie,

I have just placed a new order. Please be on time for the shipment.

Thank you.

Jimmy

親愛的潔西：

我剛下了一張新的訂單，請務必準時出貨。

謝謝！

吉米

 客戶來信：重點解讀 Getting the Hidden Messages

在我們等待把舊貨出完，好承接新單的時候，客戶沒有自己回信，而是請下屬發新訂單（以優惠價格），要我們準時出貨。可見客戶打的算盤是不要原先訂單還未出完的貨，她直接用優惠價下新單，還要求我們準時給她新貨。如果我們此時沒有深思熟慮，一旦配合客戶就完

了，客戶可能永遠不會把舊訂單的貨品出完。

　　另一方面，彼得即將到中國看我們的工廠，我們該如何掌握天時地利人和之便，要彼得履行承諾，出完舊訂單的貨呢？

● 新手任務 Your Mission:

　　即使前面我們已經打過預防針，感謝及敬佩客戶作為正直家族（honorable family）的第三代，言猶在耳，但客戶就是機關算盡。面對這樣沒信用，想占便宜的客戶，你該怎麼辦？

● 試寫Now You Try: 請試寫於下方

（試寫後才翻頁）

 教戰守則 Insider Tips

請客戶確認新訂單的日期，再次提醒要先給我們兩批貨的日期才對。

▶ 語言祕訣 Language Tips:

1. **確認正確日期**
Please confirm the correct date of the shipment for your new order.
請確認新訂單上出貨的日期是否正確。

2. **新訂單條件**
The new order will be ready to go shortly **after** we finish shipping all items on PO#2485.
新訂單等舊訂單PO#2485出貨完畢就可以開始。

3. **告知舊訂單出貨日期**
Please inform the dates for the two shipments first.
請先告知兩批貨的出貨日期。

▶ 關鍵字詞 Key Words and Phrases:
confirm (v.) 確認
correct date 正確日期
shortly (adv.) 很快地
inform (v.) 告知

我方回覆 Our Reply

Dear Jimmy,

Please confirm the correct date of the shipment for your new order. As we mentioned in our last mail, the new order will be ready to go shortly after we finish shipping all items on PO#2485. Please inform the dates for the two shipments first.

Thanks,

Jessie

親愛的吉米：

請確認新訂單上出貨的日期是否正確，我們上封郵件提到，新訂單等PO#2485所有產品出貨完畢就可以開始。請先告知兩批貨的出貨日期。

謝謝，

潔西

Round 4
第四回合

客戶來信 Letter from the Client

Jessie,

My company has not decided when to ship out PO#2485. I'll be informing you soon after I get any information.

Thanks for your patience.

Jimmy

潔西：

本公司尚未決定何時把舊訂單PO#2485出完，有消息我會很快通知你。

感謝你的耐心等待。

吉米

 客戶來信：重點解讀 Getting the Hidden Messages

客戶先用拖字訣，要我們等。

▶ 語言陷阱 Language Traps:

1. My company has not decided when to ship out PO#2485.
   本公司尚未決定何時把舊訂單PO#2485出完。

2. I'll be informing you soon after I get any information.
   有消息我會很快通知你。

▶ 技法字詞 Tricky Words and Phrases:

decide (v.) 決定

soon after 馬上，很快

🗨 新手任務 Your Mission:

面對可能出爾反爾、不守信用的回函，我們該等下去嗎？你覺得該怎麼做？

（試寫後才翻頁）

教戰守則 Insider Tips

　　為避免拖來拖去，客戶原該出貨的貨不出了，由我方主管Frank直接寫給對方可以拍板定案的主管（上駒對上駒），不要再透過下屬了。化解僵局，我方必須尋求機會。既然知道是Elaine開頭不想出完原本的訂單，這封信就該寫給另一主管（她的先生Peter）。

▶ **語言祕訣 Language Tips:**

1. **感謝新訂單**

   Thanks for your new order.
   謝謝你的新訂單。

2. **重申條件**

   Before we can move onto the new order, **we need to** finish PO#2485.
   但我們須先出完訂單PO#2485，才能著手新訂單。

3. **重申告知舊訂單出貨日期**

   Please do inform the two shipment dates for PO#2485 soon **so we can begin** to work on the new order accordingly.
   請務必告知PO#2485兩批貨的出貨日期，好讓我們依序開始新訂單。

▶ **關鍵字詞 Key Words and Phrases:**

accordingly (adv.) 依序地

信件範例 Sample Letter:

我方回覆 Our Reply

Dear Peter,

Thanks for your new order. Before we can move onto the new order, we need to finish PO#2485. Please do inform the two shipment dates for PO#2485 soon so we can begin to work on the new order accordingly.

Thanks very much!

Frank

親愛的彼得：

謝謝你的新訂單，但我們須先出完訂單PO#2485，才能著手新訂單。請務必告知PO#2485兩批貨的出貨日期，好讓我們依序開始新訂單。

非常感謝！

法蘭克

客戶來信 Letter from the Client

Frank,

OK, we will finish the two remaining shipments of PO#2485 first. Jimmy will send you the two dates shortly.

Peter

法蘭克：

好的，我們會完成PO#2485剩下的兩批貨，吉米不久就會寄給你兩個出貨的日期。

彼得

★★★★★★★★★★★★★★目標達成★★★★★★★★★★★★★★
客戶答應要把舊訂單出完，並持續新單生意。

註：客戶Peter正巧到中國出差，我方員工利用雙方員工聚餐敬酒時機，以「敬大丈夫」及「敬大丈夫一諾千金」，導引式敬酒，拱起客戶在雙方員工面前要保住顏面及誠信，再第三次敬酒「大丈夫信守承諾，先出完舊訂單，再出新訂單」，我方化解僵局，任務達成！

case 08 客戶以產地不同為由要求降價
Client Requesting Price Reduction due to Different Origin of Production

臺灣LH集團 vs 美國AUTO MASTER集團

客戶與案例背景說明
Background of the Client and the Case

　　我方接觸之窗口是美國沃爾瑪公司的採購凱瑪經理，約五十歲，大學畢，曾在Hyper market量販店（例如：Walmart沃爾瑪、Kmart凱瑪、Target目標百貨）當過採購人員，理當對於產品生產地非常熟悉。本公司在海峽兩地均有工廠，兩地也都有出貨給該公司。可是該客戶卻指責我方偷雞摸狗變更生產地，說他下訂單的產品應該是臺灣生產，而非中國製造，事實上這客戶別有用心，找個與事實不符的議題，讓工廠覺得好像發生重大的錯誤。最後目的卻是要求更改付款條件，並要求該產品降價。

Round 1
第一回合

客人來信 Letter from the Client

Dear Kate,

　　After receiving your TR-MO and AC-1876R, we have found incredible marking MADE IN CHINA on these products. It is more than a disappointment and an act of breaking promise for us. We have not

---

only lost our confidence in your company, but we are also risking ourselves for losing our customers and tarnishing our company's reputation. The reason we purchased from you was that we did not want to have the bad experience before. We changed our purchases from China to Taiwan.

Please inform in detail how you are going to correct this, how you do your quality control, and what you plan to compensate our loss for these defective items. You also need to send us a demonstration video about how to operate the items.

In addition, PO#2263 payment term will change as below:

25% down payment (already paid)

50% at sight BOL

25% three weeks after delivery for inspection

The payment of the future orders will be

20% down payment

60% at sight BOL

20% three weeks after delivery for inspection

Please let us know what you think. I'd appreciate your early response.

Nick

親愛的凱特：

收到你們的TR-MO跟AC-1876R，我們發現產品上有「中國製造」的字樣而感到無法置信。對我們而言，這不僅是失望跟違背承諾之舉，我們不僅喪失對你們公司的信任，也冒著失去我們顧客的風險以及破壞我們公司的信譽。我們向你們採購是因為不要以前不好的經

驗。我們的採購從中國改成臺灣。

請詳盡告知你現在如何把這錯誤更正，你的品質控管如何進行，以及你計畫如何賠償我們這些瑕疵品的損失。你也必須要寄給我們一個示範影帶，教我們如何操作這些產品。

另外，PO#2263付款條件會改變如下：

25%　頭期款（已付）

50%　付款交單

25%　收貨後三週檢查產品

將來訂單的付款條件為：

20%　頭期款

60%　付款交單

20%　收貨後三週檢查產品

請告訴我們你的想法，我會感謝你盡快回信。

尼克

客戶來信：重點解讀 Getting the Hidden Messages

信件看來客戶好像不要跟我們做生意了，事實並非如此。我方每方面極具競爭力，客戶雖然強烈表達不滿生產地不同，但在信尾故意露出破綻，讓我們了解他真正的用意是要求降價。

▶ **語言陷阱 Language Traps:**

1. We have found incredible marking MADE IN CHINA on these products.

   我們發現產品上有「中國製造」的字樣而感到無法置信。

2. It is more than a disappointment and an act of breaking promise

for us.

對我們而言，這不僅是失望跟違背信用之舉。

3. We have not only lost our confidence in your company, but we are also risking ourselves for losing our customers and tarnishing our company's reputation.

我們不僅喪失對你們公司的信任，也冒著失去我們顧客的風險以及破壞我們公司的信譽。

4. Please inform in detail how you are going to correct this, how you do your quality control, and what you plan to compensate our loss for these defective items.

請詳盡告知你現在如何把這錯誤更正，你的品質控管如何進行，以及你計畫如何賠償我們這些瑕疵品的損失。

5. The payment term will change as below.

付款條件會改變如下。

6. The payment of the future orders will be...

將來訂單的付款條件為……

▶ 技法字詞 Tricky Words and Phrases:

breaking promise 違背承諾

risk (v.) 冒風險

tarnish (v.) 玷汙

reputation (n.) 信譽，名聲

correct (v.) 更正

compensate (v.) 賠償

defective items 瑕疵品

客戶接二連三指責我們破壞信用，已經對我們沒信心，要我們賠償他的產品及信譽損失，要我們仔細交代解釋清楚，最後還要更改這批產品跟將來訂單的付款條件，你要怎麼回？

● 試寫Now You Try: 請試寫於下方

（試寫後才翻頁）

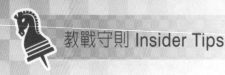
教戰守則 Insider Tips

　　客人聲東擊西，我們評估後認為可接受客人付款條件，一方面將計就計，另一方面要對客戶說明一些重點，既要彰顯跟我公司來往的都是優質客戶，也要說明我公司如何難經營，這麼做的目的在於防止客戶後續殺價。

　　處理客戶投訴（「先備知識寶典」第六項），最重要的工作如下：

1. 勇於面對客人。
2. 傾聽客人的抱怨，不要跟客人爭執。
3. 釐清問題的原因。
4. 試圖了解客戶欲解決的方式。
5. 請求給予時間再回覆解決的方式。
6. 迅速與工廠聯絡，並確認問題所在。
7. 提出我們的解決方案。
8. 與客戶磋商雙方可接受方式。
9. 迅速將問題圓滿解決。
10.將客訴問題及內容妥善記錄，供同事或其他部門參考。

接下來的工作就要按照這些原則處理，化危機為轉機。

▶ 語言祕訣 Language Tips:

　　1.　**解釋未曾通知或確認生產地**

　　　We have never informed or confirmed where our TR-MO is made.

　　　我們從未向您告知或確認TR-MO在哪裡生產。

2. **詢問資訊誤會之可能**

   Could the information **get mixed up**?
   資訊是否被混淆了？

3. **解釋人工成本大幅上漲**

   As to labor, **there is at least** 20% cost upsurge annually, **needless to mention** the ever-increasing cost of workers' social insurance.
   至於人工，每年至少上漲20%的成本，工人的社會保險不斷漲價就不須多說了。

4. **重申老顧客老價錢**

   Despite all the threats and uncertainties, we have been quoting you the same price since 2012.
   儘管面對所有威脅跟不確定性，我們從2012年到現在一直給你們相同的報價。

5. **解釋不漲價原因**

   The answer is that we want to build a long-term, well-established business relationship with you.
   那是因為我們想要跟你們建立一個可長可久的商業關係。

6. **解釋雙方遠景**

   You can easily see the fact that we have been sacrificing our company's profit for your orders **in order to sow the seeds for our common prospect**.
   我們為了你們的訂單而犧牲本公司利潤是顯而易見的，我們為了共同的將來而播種。

7. **告知隨市場調整之必要**

   The solution is that we have to adjust to the market.

答案在於我們必須因應市場調整。

8. **提出遠景**

   Our changes will be happening very soon if you kindly **keep an open door for** our cooperation in the future.

   如果你為我們的將來合作持續開門，我們的改變很快就會發生。

9. **告知我方部門同意對方條件**

   The terms of payment you proposed **have** now **been agreed** by our financial department.

   你們提出的付款條件已獲得我們的財務部門同意。

🔵 信件範例 Sample Letter:

♟ 我方發信給客戶 Our Email to the Client

Dear Nick,

We have never informed or confirmed where our TR-MO is made, but we did mention to you that our Taiwan factory manufactures industrial products for clients from all over the world, including more notably PANPAC, GOAUTO, TOPTOOL. Could the information get mixed up?

We totally understand how sensitive to price the US market is. However, it is equally important to have both price and quality competitiveness. We have been facing all kinds of cost soaring--land, rent, material, and shipment, and so on. As to labor, there is at least 20% cost upsurge annually, needless to mention the ever-increasing cost of workers'social insurance. Despite all the threats and uncertainties, we have been quoting you the same price since 2012.

Why do we have to keep the price the same, and how do we do it? The answer is that we want to build a long-term, well-established business relationship with you. You can easily see the fact that we have been sacrificing our company's profit for your orders in order to sow the seeds for our common prospect.

The solution is that we have to adjust to the market. First, increase the price, which could be the least desirable for your company. Second, use robots to replace workers. It will take a long time, but we have already stepped in the process. (Ref. our robot welding https://www.youtube.com/watch?v=btwypaqYj3). Third, change human resource structure by cutting down the number of workers. For example, instead of hiring four people, paying four salaries, for four job loads, we plan to hire only two workers, to work double load, and pay three salaries.

In short, the disadvantaged positions are clearing out. Our changes will be happening very soon if you kindly keep an open door for our cooperation in the future.

Meanwhile, the terms of payment you proposed have now been agreed by our financial department.

Best regards,

Frank

親愛的尼克：

我們從未向您告知或確認TR-MO在哪裡生產，但我們確實跟您提過本公司的臺灣廠生產工業用產品，客戶來自全世界，包括知名的「泛太平洋」（PANPAC）、「自動運轉」（GOAUTO）、「上頂工

具」（TOPTOOL）。資訊是否被混淆了？

我們了解美國市場對價格有多敏感，但是價格跟品質兩者競爭力同樣重要。我們面對所有的成本上揚──土地、租金、原物料以及運費等。至於人工，每年至少上漲20%的成本，工人的社會保險不斷漲價就不須多說了。儘管面對所有的威脅跟不確定性，我們從2012年到現在一直給你們相同的報價。

我們為什麼要保持相同價格，我們又是怎麼辦到的？那是因為我們想要跟你們建立一個可長可久的商業關係。我們為了你們的訂單而犧牲本公司利潤是顯而易見的，我們為了共同的將來而播種。

答案在於我們必須因應市場調整。首先，我們必須漲價，那是貴公司所最不樂見的。第二，用機器人來代替工人。那會花上一段長時間，但我們已經進入那階段（請參考我們youtube影片的機器焊接）。第三，以減少工人來改變人力資源結構。舉例來說，請四個人，付四份薪水，做四個人的工作，我們打算請兩個人，做雙倍工作，付三個人的薪水。

簡而言之，不利的因素正在被清除，如果你為我們的將來合作持續開門，我們的改變很快就會發生。

同時，你們提出的付款條件已獲得我們的財務部門同意。

誠摯祝福，

法蘭克

▶ **關鍵字詞 Key Words and Phrases:**

sensitive (adj.) 敏感的

competitiveness (n.) 競爭力

cost soaring 成本高漲

upsurge (n.) 上漲

threats and uncertainties 威脅與不確定

sow the seeds 播種

disadvantaged positions 不利因素

open door 開門

Round 2
第二回合

 客戶回信 Client's Reply

Dear Frank,

Thanks for the reply. Your company and bank information are both in Taiwan. What should we expect? We have been receiving quality products from you until this time. I expect nothing less, so please verify that the products are taking all necessary quality control steps.

We have finished inspecting AC-1876R today. We like the packaging and the product, but I need you to put our logo on the packaging and the manual. There is one problem we found on AC-1876R. There are no holes on the rack. We can drill the holes by ourselves, but the cost will be deducted from the payment. Please confirm.

Besides, thanks for agreeing with the changes of the payment terms.

Nick

親愛的法蘭克：

謝謝你的回信，貴公司跟銀行都在臺灣，你要我們怎麼想？我們持續收到你們有品質的產品，一直到這次為止。我的期待不會減少，所以請確認產品經過所有的品質控管步驟。

我們今天完成檢驗AC-1876R，我們喜歡包裝跟產品，但我需

要你們放我們的標誌在包裝跟手冊上。我們發現AC-1876R有一個問題，架子沒有打洞，我們可以自己鑽洞，但是成本要從付款中扣除，請確認。

另外，謝謝你們同意付款條件的改變。

尼克

客戶來信：重點解讀 Getting the Hidden Messages

客戶事實上已達到他的目的，我們已經同意他所要求改變的付款條件，但信中他還是要表示他沒說謊以及他對於認知產品製造地的不愉快。對於我方產品有褒有貶，重點是客戶藉此要求好品質及我方必須配合他要求的事項。

▶ **語言陷阱 Language Traps:**

1. What should we expect?
   你要我們怎麼想？

2. I expect nothing less, so please verify that the products are taking all necessary quality control process.
   我的期待不會減少，所以請確認產品經過所有的品質控管步驟。

▶ **技法字詞 Tricky Words and Phrases:**

expect (v.) 期待
verify (v.) 確認

新手任務 Your Mission:
這封信要處理的問題有兩個：

1. 我方生意難做可能賠錢，還須符合客戶要求的好品質。
2. 客戶仍爲生產地爲中國，而非臺灣感到不悅。

你要怎麼回信？

● 試寫Now You Try: 請試寫於下方

（試寫後才翻頁）

　　我方回信還是要繼續強調成本高漲，讓客戶了解我們面臨價格競爭又要求好品質所面臨的挑戰。另外，我們願意賠給他新的產品，一來消除他的不愉快；再者，我們希望他能增加對我們採購產品的數量。

▶ 語言祕訣 Language Tips:

1. 檢討自己

Our recent performance must have lost some trust on your side.

我們最近的表現一定讓你們失去信心了。

2. 感謝客戶包容（且暗示我們的努力）

Please kindly do bear with us since we are really trying very hard to find the solution for every aspect no matter what the causes are.

你們慷慨地忍受我們為每個方面尋求解決的極度努力，無論原因為何。

3. 解釋利潤損失

We have to deal with price competition under this long period of stagnation which has caused our factory's **profit loss significantly**.

我們必須面對長期停滯的價格競爭而造成的龐大利潤損失。

4. 說明負責瑕疵品

We have no excuse but to take all the responsibility for the defect issues.

我們沒有藉口，只有對瑕疵品負全責。

5. **未來之展望**

It is our greatest hope that the new production line can bring more success business and benefit to you!

我們衷心希望新的生產線能帶給你們更多生意跟利益！

信件範例 Sample Letter:

我方發信給客戶 Our Email to the Client

Dear Nick,

Our recent performance must have lost some trust on your side; please kindly do bear with us since we are really trying very hard to find the solution for every aspect no matter what the causes are.

We have been facing several challenges. First, we have to deal with price competition under this long period of stagnation which has caused our factory's profit loss significantly. Second, our workers come and go so frequently as if we were training school interns, because their low wages do not even allow them to make a living. All our efforts to train and invest in our workers have gone into the drain again and again.

We have no excuse but to take all the responsibility for the defect issues. As a result, we need to increase the training budget to improve competencies of our employees in the short term.

We are very serious to your second chance of the new order for nothing can be wrong. Our changes will be happening very soon if you kindly keep an open door for our cooperation in the future.

Meanwhile, we will load 10 pieces of TR-MO for free, with your order PO#2268, for you to develop new production line. It is our greatest hope that the new production line can bring more success business and benefit to you!

Best,

Frank

親愛的尼克：

　　我們最近的表現一定讓你們失去信心了，你們慷慨地忍受我們為每個方面尋求解決的極度努力，無論原因為何。

　　我們一直面對好幾個挑戰。首先，我們必須面對長期停滯的價格競爭而造成的龐大利潤損失。再者，我們的工人來來去去如此頻繁，好像我們是在訓練學校的實習生一樣，因為他們的工資低到根本不足以維生。我們的努力訓練與投資一次次地被白白浪費。

　　我們沒有藉口，只有對瑕疵品負全責。所以我們需要增加訓練經費，以在短期內增加員工的能力。

　　我們對你們給新訂單的再次機會非常慎重，因為沒有什麼能出錯了。如果你好心地為我們的將來合作持續開一扇門，我們的改變很快就會發生。

　　同時，我們在訂單PO#2268會裝10臺免費的TR-MO給你們發展新生產線。我們衷心希望新的生產線能帶給你們更多生意跟利益！

　　誠摯祝福，

　　法蘭克

▶ 關鍵字詞 Key Words and Phrases:

trust (n.) 信任

bear (v.) 忍受

challenge (n.) 挑戰

stagnation (n.) 停滯

keep an open door 留一扇門

★★★★★★★★★★★★★★目標達成★★★★★★★★★★★★★★

客戶願意接受品質穩固之中國製產品，持續與我方生意往來。

case 09 客戶被詐騙卻要求供應商出貨
Client Demanding Delivery of Products after a Fraud

臺灣LH集團 VS 澳洲OUTWINNER進口商

客戶與案例背景說明
Background of the Client and the Case

　　這是一個國際詐騙的事件，受害者是我方澳洲籍的客戶，但這客戶意圖把責任推給本公司的員工，負擔他的損失。這澳洲客戶大約四十歲，雪梨大學體育系畢業，熱愛修理機械。與本公司往來約六至七年，每年約進口五至六櫃本公司產品，並直接使用本公司的產品影片作爲他網頁向消費者介紹產品的廣告。因爲公司地址設爲郵政信箱，並非一般有地址的公司行號，與本公司的生意往來都是100%付款後，我們才會出貨。

事發原由

　　客戶聲稱被網路詐騙兩萬多美金，他用電話告知我方員工，但我方員工在談話中無意說出「也許我的電腦也被駭了」，客戶就抓住這一點，說本公司的員工害他被騙，要本公司跟他共同承擔損失。

 客戶來信 Letter from the Client

Dear Frank,

We have always cooperated with LH well for many years. Recently we have paid for our new order in advance as asked. The payment to the bank is on the invoice (see attachment).

It was such a shock for us to find that your employee Nina's computer has doubtlessly been hacked. The leak and the interception of the bank information between our emails have now made us the victims of a fraud. We paid as asked this time and have done exactly the same transaction as in the past. We believed it was your company's invoice and considered that the delivery would go as usual.

Our company is having an IT security team investigate this case. The full report will serve as the evidence in any legal actions later.

Please inform how you plan to deal with this matter. We need to be sure that we get our order and continue our business with you.

The emails between Nina and my company can be sent to you if necessary. We hope to resolve the matter by our mutual agreement without involving any legal proceedings.

Best regards,

Ben

親愛的法蘭克：

我們與LH許多年來都合作無間，最近我們按照你們的要求，預先為我們的訂單付款。

我們很震驚地發現貴公司員工妮娜的電腦毫無疑問地被駭了，我們郵件中的銀行資訊被洩露跟攔截，現在造成我們成為詐騙的受害者。我們按照發票要求付款，這次同樣按照以前一樣完成交易，我們認為那是你們公司的發票，並且認為我們會像以往一樣收到貨物。

我們的公司現在請一組資訊安全人員調查這個案件，詳盡報告會作為將來法律行動的證據。

請告知你將會如何處理這件事，我們需要確信我們能收到貨，並且繼續跟你們做生意。

有必要的話，妮娜跟我們公司的郵件可以寄給你。我希望以我們雙方同意的辦法來解決這件事，不需要牽扯到任何法律的程序。

誠摯祝福，

班

客戶來信：重點解讀 Getting the Hidden Messages

客人信中一口咬定是本公司員工害他被騙，還暗示會用法律來解決這事情，但客戶信中所給的資料無法顯示本公司與他被騙有關。

▶ 語言陷阱 Language Traps:

1. We have always cooperated with LH well for many years.
   我們與LH許多年來都合作無間。

2. It was such a shock for us to find that your employee Nina's computer has doubtlessly been hacked.
   我們很震驚地發現貴公司員工妮娜的電腦毫無疑問地被駭了。

3. The leak and the interception of the bank information between our emails have now made us the victims of a fraud.

我們郵件中的銀行資訊被洩露跟攔截，現在造成我們成為詐騙的受害者。

4. We paid as asked this time and have done exactly the same transaction as in the past.
我們按照你們的要求付款，這次同樣按照以前一樣完成交易。

5. Our company is having an IT security team investigate this case. The full report will serve as the evidence in any legal actions later.
我們的公司現在請一組資訊安全人員調查這個案件，詳盡報告會作為將來法律行動的證據。

6. Please inform how you plan to deal with this matter.
請告知你將會如何處理這件事。

7. We need to be sure that we get our order and continue our business with you.
我們需要確信我們能收到貨，並且繼續跟你們做生意。

8. We hope to resolve the matter by our mutual agreement without involving any legal proceedings.
我希望以我們雙方同意的辦法來解決這件事，不需要牽扯到任何法律的程序。

▶ 技法字詞 Tricky Words and Phrases:
cooperate (v.) 合作
invoice (n.) 發票
doubtlessly (adv.) 無疑地
hack (v.) 駭
leak (v.) 洩露

interception (n.) 攔截

fraud (n.) 詐騙

legal proceedings 法律程序

● 新手任務 Your Mission:

老闆要你先寫回信的草稿。你該怎麼回？

● 試寫 Now You Try: 請試寫於下方

（試寫後才翻頁）

教戰守則 Insider Tips

　　為了跟客人維持關係，也為了保護我們自己，我們必須報警（如資料不足可能無法取得報案文件，但必須取得報案時間、報警單位與受理警員名字）。如無法於報警電話取得資料，須由員工親至警察單位報警，並將客戶提供的被詐騙資料交予警方。

　　回信重點：主管不會親自回這封信，而是讓屬下或公司法務部回信（見以下信件），以減低其衝擊，但主管一定會先看過草稿，防止錯誤。這封信的你／我務必分清楚，我們一定要置身事外，不要被牽扯進來。

▶ 語言祕訣 Language Tips:

1. **表達遺憾及告知採取之行動**

   We feel sorry about your online fraud and **have reported to** the police about your case.

   我們為你們遭到網路詐騙感到難過，也把這個案子報警了。

2. **告知警方說明**

   The police have indicated that it is an international fraud based on your incomplete evidence.

   依照你們不完整的資訊，警察指出這是國際詐騙。

3. **告知警方將發出聲明**

   China's International Police Agency **will issue a "notice" to** Australia related units that include all customs, taxes, the local police, and other coordinating authorities.

   「中國國際警署」會發給澳洲相關單位（包含所有海關、稅務機關、當地警察以及其他配合的權責單位）一個聲明。

4. 告知我方處置貨物方式

Before the situation gets cleared out, **we will hold the goods until** we receive the official final report from the International Police.

在情況明朗前，我們會保管貨品，直到我們收到國際警察最後的官方報告為止。

▶ 關鍵字詞 Key Words and Phrases:

report to the police 報案

incomplete evidence 不完整資訊

issue a "notice" 發出「聲明」

clear out 清楚，明朗

hold the goods until 保管貨物直到

● 信件範例 Sample Letter:

我方發信給客戶 Our Email to the Client

Hi, Ben,

We feel sorry about your online fraud and have reported to the police about your case. The police have indicated that it is an international fraud based on your incomplete evidence. China's International Police Agency will issue a "notice" to Australia related units that include all customs, taxes, the local police, and other coordinating authorities.

Before the situation gets cleared out, we will hold the goods until we receive the official final report from the International Police.

Best regards,

Nina

嗨，班：

我們為你們遭到網路詐騙感到難過，也把這個案子報警了。依照你們不完整的資訊，警察指出這是國際詐騙。「中國國際警署」會發給澳洲相關單位（包含所有海關、稅務機關、當地警察以及其他配合的權責單位）一個聲明。

在情況明朗前，我們會保管貨品，直到我們收到國際警察最後的官方報告為止。

誠摯祝福，

妮娜

Round 2
第二回合

 客戶回信 Client's Reply

Dear Nina,

Your company should share in the losses.

Best,

Ben

親愛的妮娜：

貴公司應該分攤我們的損失。

誠摯祝福，

班

客戶來信：重點解讀 Getting the Hidden Messages

　　客戶這封信說得很直白，要求我們分攤損失。世界上沒有任何機構能防止被駭，每個人都必須要有警覺。客戶遭詐騙後的求償對象，當然是警方辦案查出之詐騙罪犯，與本公司無關。

　　雖然客戶不太可能自導自演，然而無論如何，通知客戶我們已經報警是必要的，也表示我們站在他那邊。但客戶要領貨，必須付貨款給我們。客戶聲稱已經付款給詐騙集團，要領走我們的貨，或是要我們負擔他被詐騙的金額，這些都是不合理的要求。

新手任務 Your Mission:
你如何回應客戶分攤損失的要求？

試寫Now You Try: 請試寫於下方

　　（試寫後才翻頁）

不跟隨客戶起舞，也不要跟客戶辯駁這種可能無中生有的事，輕描淡寫爲上策。無論客戶怎麼說，一切要等官方調查有結果再說。

▶ 語言祕訣 Language Tips:

1. **再次表示遺憾**

   We are sorry again for what has happened to you.
   我們爲你所發生的情形再次感到遺憾。

2. **重申等待官方結果**

   We will not know our next step **until the result of the official investigation is clear to us**.
   在我們清楚了解官方調查結果之前，我們不會知道要採取什麼步驟。

▶ 關鍵字詞 Key Words and Phrases:

official investigation 官方調查

● 信件範例 Sample Letter:

🐴 我方發信給客戶 Our Email to the Client

Hi, Ben,

　　We are sorry again for what has happened to you. We will not know our next step until the result of the official investigation is clear to us.

Best,

Nina

嗨，班：

我們為你所發生的情形再次感到遺憾，在我們清楚了解官方調查結果之前，我們不會知道要採取什麼步驟。

誠摯祝福，

妮娜

🗨 重要聲明

我方不久後發出聲明給其他的客戶：注意網路詐騙，注意匯款資料的填寫，但不要在信中提到本公司已有客戶被騙，以免造成其他客戶害怕跟我方交易。

♞ 緊急聲明 Urgent Statement

Dear Customers,

Today, we are convinced that fraud is rampant in the world. A hacker probably counterfeited our company name to create a fraudulent email account and a fake bank account. To absolutely protect your company payment, please always be alert to our correct bank account. Check with us the correct bank account EVERY TIME BEFORE you remit any payment to our company.

Best wishes,

LH Group

親愛的客戶：

今天我們了解到世界上詐騙的猖獗。有駭客可能偽造我們公司的名字，建立了假的郵件帳號以及一個假的銀行帳號。為了完全保護你們的公司付款，請一直保持對我們的銀行帳號的警惕。當你們要匯款給本公司前，務必再跟本公司確認匯款帳號。

誠摯祝福，

LH集團

客戶一陣子沒來信

Round 3
第三回合

客戶來信 Letter from the Client

Dear Nina,

Can you please quote for my inquiry? For detailed information, please add another column to show the part numbers with the items.

Thanks for the help.

Barbara

親愛的妮娜：

請幫我詢問報價，為了詳細資料起見，請加欄位顯示零件編號與項目。

謝謝你的幫忙。

芭芭拉

Dear Barbara,

Please see the attachment for a better chart. Do let me know if there are any questions.

Best Regards,

Nina

親愛的芭芭拉：

請看附件有一個比較好的圖表，讓我知道是不是有任何問題。

誠摯祝福，

妮娜

Round 4
第四回合

客戶來信 Letter from the Client

Hi, Nina,

Please find signed order in the attachment. I'm having my motor-cycle trip in the US. You can see the photos on my Instagram.

Regards,

Ben

嗨，妮娜：

請看附件已經簽名的訂單。我現正在美國騎車旅行，你可以看我Instagram的照片。

誠摯祝福，

班

♞ 我方回覆Our Reply

Hi, Ben,

The order has been received. Thanks!

How is your motorcycle trip? Any interesting experience?

Best regards,

Nina

嗨，班：

訂單收到了，感謝！

你的重機之旅如何？有任何有趣的經驗嗎？

誠摯祝福，

妮娜

★★★★★★★★★★★★★目標達成★★★★★★★★★★★★★

我們堅持客人付完貨款才出那批貨，並有心理打算如客人不付款，我們自行處理。結果兩三週後，客人就付款了。

客戶半年後又下訂單，沒再提詐騙索賠，持續與我們生意往來。

業務不是工程師的翻譯
Agents Are Not Engineers' Translators

臺灣LH集團 vs 美國EASY MACHINE SHOP集團

客戶與案例背景說明
Background of the Client and the Case

美國中部密西根的老客戶，曾任職於機械行業全球最大之公司擔任高級管理，往來臺灣及中國數十年，可說是臺灣通及中國通。對產品要求嚴格，合約規範之產品不容許私自修改規格。

此次案件工廠未提前通知客戶就更動產品的設計，當然不對，客戶生氣來信要求解釋，但助理的第一封回覆卻已經讓客戶動怒。客戶連寫了兩三封回信想知道到底是怎麼回事，助理的回覆只讓客人愈來愈氣。助理該怎樣扮好角色，作為工程師與客戶的溝通橋梁？

Round 1
第一回合

● 新手任務 Your Mission:

工廠未通知就修改零件，先斬後奏，茲事體大，我們得知後發信給客戶說明，並尋求同意。

● 試寫Now You Try: 請試寫於下方

（試寫後才翻頁）

Dear Robert,

Please note that one washer will be placed on the valve of the gas pump for pressure stabilization. The drawing of this part is as below.

The change will start from the last shipment of PO#1783 and the first shipment of PO#1805. The items will be tested before delivery. Both shipments will be sent out at the end of Sep.

We are sorry for not informing you earlier and hope that you accept the change.

Best,

Kelly

親愛的羅伯:

請注意有一個墊圈會被放到瓦斯幫浦的閥門上以增加壓力的穩定。這部分的圖示如下。

PO#1783的最後一批貨與PO#1805的第一批貨就會開始這個改變,產品會測試後再行運送,這兩批貨會在9月底會出貨。

我們很抱歉沒有早點告訴你,希望你接受這個改變。

誠摯祝福,

凱莉

(註:助理信件文法錯誤已經修改過。)

找出問題 Finding the Problems

你看到助理這封信有什麼問題？你能找出有問題的語句嗎？

如果你是客戶，訂貨被更改，你的供應商先斬後奏，你的反應為何？

語言問題 Language Problems:

1. Please note that one washer will be placed on the valve of the gas pump for pressure stabilization.（請注意有一個墊圈會被放到瓦斯幫浦的閥門上以增加壓力的穩定。）

2. The change will start from the last shipment of PO#1783 and the first shipment of PO#1805.（PO#1783的最後一批貨與PO#1805的第一批貨就會開始這個改變。）

3. We are sorry for not informing you earlier and hope that you accept the change.（我們很抱歉沒有早點告知你，希望你接受這個改變。）

地雷字詞 Words and Phrases to Avoid:

note (v.) 注意

inform (v.) 通知

accept (v.) 接受

🗨 助理信件分析Analyzing the Assistant's Letter:

我們可以預見這封信將帶給客戶的衝擊，貨物未經同意已經被更改，出貨時間也箭在弦上，「我們很抱歉沒有早點告知你，希望你接受這個改變。」助理的寫法恐怕是太天真了，一秒惹毛客戶，因為貨物更改牽扯的後續問題非常多。先斬後奏絕對是行不通的，造成的時間與成本誰來買單？

Kelly,

The factory MUST answer my questions:

1. Why did the factory make this change?

2. Was the change related to the bad springs that have caused reading errors?

I'm not happy. I have test facilities and we will test. Both questions must be answered before our testing or approval.

Robert Johnson

凱莉：

工廠必須回答我的問題：

1. 為什麼工廠要做這個更改？

2. 這個改變跟壞彈簧造成幫浦數據出錯有關嗎？

我很不開心。我有測試機具，我們會測試。在測試與同意前，這兩個問題都必須要回答。

羅伯強森

客戶來信：重點解讀 Getting the Hidden Messages

客人回信直接說他很不高興，並且要工廠回答他的提問，顯然助理所寫的內容不但沒幫助，反而讓他搞糊塗，客戶會狐疑工廠的動機是否在偷工減料。他在信尾留了伏筆，如果工廠先斬後奏沒能提出讓他滿意的理由，他不但有測試的機器，還有可能拒絕收貨！

▶ 客戶用語表達 Client's Expressions:

1. The factory MUST answer my questions.
   工廠必須回答我的問題。

2. I'm not happy. I have test facilities and we will test.
   我很不開心。我有測試機具，我們會測試。

3. Both questions must be answered before our testing or approval.
   在測試與同意前，這兩個問題都必須要回答。

▶ 技法字詞 Tricky Words and Phrases:

test facilities 測試機具

approval (n.) 同意

Round 2
第二回合

🔵 新手任務 Your Mission:

　　客戶不明白工廠為何胡搞他訂的產品，很生氣地要工廠好好解釋。如果你是這個案子的助理，工廠告訴你原因，你該怎麼溝通讓客戶了解？

🔵 試寫Now You Try: 請試寫於下方

_____

_____

_____

_____

（試寫後才翻頁）

我方助理寫給客戶 Our Assistant's Letter to the Client

Robert,

The factory has answered your questions.

The valve of the new spring came to the thread at 6/10-12 UNC. Because the thread could not hold the bolts tightly, it was punched. After the factory changed the thread to 6/12-14 UNF and added one washer, the punch was not necessary anymore. Also, the time for pressure regulating has been reduced from 30 minutes to 25 minutes.

Please let us know if you have any questions.

Best regards,

Kelly

羅伯：

工廠回答了你的問題。

新的彈簧閥門為6/10-12 UNC ，因為螺紋無法栓緊，所以螺紋要被敲打過。在工廠改變螺紋到6/12-14 UNF後，加上一個墊圈，就不需要敲打了。還有，壓力調節的時間從30分鐘減少為25分鐘。

如果你有任何疑問，請讓我們知道。

誠摯祝福，

凱莉

 ## 找出問題 Finding the Problems

先斬後奏是違反合約的行為，如果客人拒收貨物，對我們求償，我方將損失慘重。助理再次寫出有問題的信件，簡直是提油救火，讓客戶更憤怒！

究竟助理的角色是什麼？信件要傳達給客戶什麼資訊？這些螺紋名詞UNC（United National Coarse）與UNF（United National Fine）須先了解清楚。了解產品更動的細節後，是否就能按照工程師的話逐字翻譯，認為客人就會懂，就會接受我們未經他同意擅自作主的更改？擔任溝通橋梁的人如果沒弄懂如何連結雙方，必定造成溝通不良，帶來更多誤解。

　　仔細看哪些是有問題的語句，跟客戶講改來改去的細節有必要嗎？壓力調節的時間減少是客戶要求的嗎？到底更改設計的根本原因是什麼？怎麼寫才能反轉情勢，讓客戶看到的不是麻煩，而是利多？

語言問題 Language Problems:

1. 因為螺紋無法栓緊，所以螺紋要被敲打過。

   Because the thread could not hold the bolts tightly, it was punched.

2. 在工廠改變螺紋到6/12-14 UNF後，加上一個墊圈，就不需要敲打了。

   After the factory changed the thread to 6/12-14 UNF and added one washer, the punch was not necessary anymore.

地雷字詞 Words and Phrases to Avoid:

punch (v.) 敲打

add (v.) 添加

💬 助理信件分析 Analyzing the Assistant's Letter:

　　客戶讀到「因為螺紋無法栓緊，所以螺紋要被敲打過。」可能會無法呼吸，因為螺紋最怕的就是撞擊，工廠竟然還敲打過。後來沒敲打了，可是又加了零件，對客戶來說這些莫名其妙、不知所為何來的程序，通通在找他麻煩。

客戶回信 Client's Reply

> Kelly,
>
> The factory is creating another problem. The changes are made WITHOUT our approval. The cost could be a big waste of time and money. There was no need for any change at all with the correct spring being used.
>
> Robert

凱莉：

工廠在製造另一個問題，這些改變沒有經過我們的允許，這可能會花掉我們一大堆時間跟金錢。用正確的彈簧，沒有必要做任何改變。

羅伯

 客戶來信：重點解讀 Getting the Hidden Messages

助理沒有從客戶的角度想，改變對客戶有何意義？客人失去耐性了，這些改變只是讓他討厭，多出成本跟風險，或許更改設計後的品質堪慮。因此，他要求工廠用正確的零件做出貨品，拒絕突如其來的改變。

▶ 客戶用語表達 Client's Expressions:

1. The factory is creating another problem.

   工廠在製造另一個問題。

2. The changes are made WITHOUT our approval.

   這些改變沒有經過我們的允許。

3. The cost could be a big waste of time and money.

   這可能會花掉我們一大堆時間跟金錢。

4. There was no need for any change at all with the correct spring being used.

   用正確的彈簧，沒有必要做任何改變。

▶ 關鍵字詞 Key Words and Phrases:

create another problem 製造問題

big waste 浪費

correct spring 正確的彈簧

Round 3
第三回合

客戶再度來信 Another Letter from the Client

Kelly,

I'm not interested in fighting with the factory. All I'm asking is understanding, to have consistent, good quality products for my customers. The factory did not answer my questions in the previous mail--

1. Why did the factory make this change?

2. Was the change related to the bad springs that have caused reading errors?

If we have good springs, the readings will be correct. It seems that the factory changed the thread in order to adjust the pressure settings, right? I'm confused. This is like chicken and eggs. What comes first? Please answer my questions.

Robert

凱莉：

我沒興趣跟工廠爭辯，我只是要求理解，能給我的顧客一致的、好的產品，工廠並沒有回答我上封信的問題——

1. 爲什麼要改？

2. 這個改變跟差勁的彈簧造成幫浦數據出錯有關嗎？

如果我們有好的彈簧，讀數會正確的。看起來工廠是爲了調整壓力設定而改變螺紋，對嗎？我搞不清楚，現在是雞生蛋還是蛋生雞？請回答我的問題。

羅伯

 客戶來信：重點解讀 Getting the Hidden Messages

客戶對於助理直接翻譯工程師的技術說明無法理解，所以客戶重複提到「用好的彈簧，數據就會正確，產品就不用修改」。客戶也認爲工廠跟作爲供應商的我方完全不理解他必須提供給消費者可靠產品的立場。雖然如此，客戶還是再給我們一次機會說明。

▶ 客戶用語表達 Client's Expressions:

1. I'm not interested in fighting with the factory.
   我沒興趣跟工廠爭辯。

2. All I'm asking is understanding, to have consistent, good quality products for my customers.

我只是要求理解，能給我的顧客一致的、好的產品。

3. The factory did not answer my questions in the previous mail.

工廠並沒有回答我上封信的問題。

4. If we have good springs, the readings will be correct.

如果我們有好的彈簧，讀數會正確的。

5. I'm confused. This is like chicken and eggs. What comes first?

我搞不清楚，現在是雞生蛋還是蛋生雞？

▶ **關鍵字詞** Key Words and Phrases:

understanding (n.) 理解

consistent (adj.) 一致的

chicken and eggs 雞生蛋還是蛋生雞

🔵 新手任務 Your Mission:

客戶再度給我們一次機會說明到底更改設計是為了什麼？如果我們再搞不清楚怎麼說才能讓他理解接受，並幫他處理因此產生的問題，恐怕我們就要負責賠償了。

🔵 試寫 Now You Try: 請試寫於下方

（試寫後才翻頁）

教戰守則 Insider Tips

　　如果助理在第一時間就了解最需要告知的重點是什麼，客戶或許就不會動怒。我們必須自問：為什麼他要接受我們先斬後奏？他是客戶，為何要配合我們？我們因此給他帶來一堆麻煩，對他有什麼好處？你又如何消除他的疑慮？

　　首先，先斬後奏就是違背合約，我們必須認錯，先消客戶的氣。最重要的是要從客戶的觀點看問題，解決他的疑惑或因此產生的麻煩，用他能了解並且想要聽到的語言來溝通說服，我們要給客戶的是動力（他將獲利或產品因此更強大），而非壓力。助理弄錯重點，直接翻譯轉述工程師的數字或技術，反而愈幫愈忙激怒客戶，除非客戶也是工程師出身，那就另當別論。

　　業務或助理可不是工程師請來的翻譯，更改項目列出或備註即可，不必畫蛇添足多加解釋，工程的枝微末節客戶不需要了解。真正的重點不在於一五一十告訴客戶怎麼更改，為何更改，而在於我們怎麼設身處地透過合適的語言、恰當的說法，擔任溝通的橋梁，跟客戶溝通，讓客戶理解更改能帶給他什麼利多（而不是麻煩），才能說服客戶，化險為夷。（比較助理與經理的信件。）

▶ 語言祕訣 Language Tips：

1. 承認錯誤

   It is not right to have changed the design of the product without informing the client.

   工廠未提前通知客戶就更動產品的設計，這是不對的。

2. 解釋原因

   There are two reasons behind.

改變閥的設計的原因有二。

3. **告知利多**

   The above changes do not affect the quality. Instead, it **enhances the stability**.

   以上的改變並不會影響品質，反而能提高品質的穩定度。

4. **請求原諒及確認接受（優化之）修改**

   Please understand the improving changes **and confirm your acceptance**.

   請原諒工廠對於閥體的改變，並請確認接受更改。

5. **請求空運樣品確認**

   If you wish, the factory can send two products with the changes **for your confirmation**.

   如果你需要，工廠可先空運兩件更改後的閥體給你確認。

● 信件範例 Sample Letter:

我方經理回信 Our Manager's Letter to the Client

Dear Robert,

It is not right to have changed the design of the product without informing the client. There are two reasons behind:

1. To increase the life of the valve and the spring.
2. To precisely adjust the pressure of the valve as required.

The above changes do not affect the quality. Instead, it enhances the stability. The two changes are:

1. The thread has been changed from 6/10-12 UNC to 6/12-14 UNF.

2. An adjustable outer circle has been fixed onto the valve.

Please understand the improving changes and confirm your acceptance. If you wish, the factory can send two products with the changes for your confirmation.

Best regards,

Frank

親愛的羅伯：

工廠未提前通知客戶就更動產品的設計，這是不對的。

改變閥的設計的原因有二：

1. 增加閥體及彈簧的使用壽命。

2. 按照要求，更精準地調整閥的壓力。

以上的改變並不會影響品質，反而能提高品質的穩定度。

兩個改變的部分為：

1. 螺牙從6/10-12 UNC改成6/12-14 UNF。

2. 在閥體外加上一個固定且可調整的外環。

請原諒工廠對於閥體的改變，並請確認接受更改。如果你需要，工廠可先空運兩件更改後的閥體給你確認。

法蘭克

▶ 關鍵字詞 Key Words and Phrases:

increase the life 增加使用壽命

enhance the stability 提高品質穩定度

the improving changes 有益的改變

新手任務 Your Mission:

　　客戶一段時間沒回應,也不表態是否需要我們寄兩個產品過去,可能氣憤未消,也可能要更多時間思考,你該怎麼做?

試寫Now You Try: 請試寫於下方

_____

_____

_____

_____

_____

_____

_____

_____

_____

_____

_____

_____

_____

_____

（試寫後才翻頁）

教戰守則 Insider Tips

　　不必再等，寄出隔天抵達的快遞（overnight delivery）產品給客戶測試好解決他的疑慮，請他回覆你測試結果，就知道客戶對這批貨的態度了。當然快遞貨號跟預計抵達日期要給客戶，你還要盤算如何處理接下來的幾個可能性（接受／有條件接受／拒絕），客戶既不能因此增加成本，我們也不能賠錢，但一切後續仍要等到客戶測試結果才能明朗。

▶ 語言祕訣 Language Tips:

1. **告知已寄出產品供評估**

   To help you make a decision, we now send you two products with the changes for your evaluation (FedEx tracking No. 1058 1316 2207).

   爲了讓你方便下決定，我們現在寄出兩個改過的產品讓你評估（聯邦快遞追蹤號碼1058 1316 2207）。

2. **請求告知收到及測試結果**

   Please let us know if you receive the parcel and the result of your test.

   請讓我們知道你是否收到包裹，以及你測試的結果。

▶ 關鍵字詞 Key Words and Phrases:

to help you make a decision 爲了方便你下決定

parcel (n.) 包裹

the result of your test 你測試的結果

🐴 我方發信給客戶 Our Email to the Client

Dear Robert,

We have not received your words for a while. To help you make a decision, we now send you two products with the changes for your evaluation (FedEx tracking No. 1058 1316 2207). The parcel should arrive overnight.

Please let us know if you receive the parcel and the result of your test.

Best regards,

Kelly

親愛的羅伯：

我們有一陣子沒收到你的回覆了，為了讓你方便下決定，我們現在寄出兩個改過的產品讓你評估（聯邦快遞追蹤號碼1058 1316 2207）。包裹應該隔天就會收到。

請讓我們知道你是否收到包裹，以及你測試的結果。

誠摯祝福，

凱莉

🐴 客戶回信 Client's Reply

Kelly,

We have evaluated the two valves with good quality springs side by side. There is no difference between the two valves readings. However, there are a lot of issues that come with the factory's making the changes without our approval first.

1. The spring is changed, the height and the diameter.
2. The installation and adjustment procedures will be different.
3. Owner's manuals will have to be changed.
4. Without the end customer's approval, this change could disqualify us as a supplier.
5. What did the factory do to qualify the new design?
6. How many cycles has the factory gone through?
7. What extra costs were incurred because of the change?

No, I will not accept the change. Future shipments will be rejected for not having our approval in advance.

Robert Johnson

凱莉：

我們已經並排測試了兩個有好彈簧的閥體，兩者的數據並無差異，但是工廠沒有我們的同意任意做改變，帶來許多的問題。

1. 彈簧被改了，高度跟直徑。
2. 安裝跟調整步驟會不一樣。
3. 使用手冊也要改。
4. 沒有消費者的認可，我們可能變成不合格的供應商。
5. 工廠做了什麼來保證新設計的品質？
6. 工廠經過多少次重複的過程讓這個更改合理？
7. 因為這改變而多出來的成本是多少？

不，我不會接受更改。你們將來的出貨不會被接受，因為沒有經過我們事先的同意。

羅伯強森

客戶來信：重點解讀 Getting the Hidden Messages

　　客戶沒有對新設計不高興，但他在意新設計的品質以及衍生的出來的諸多問題，這些才是他拒絕接受更改的原因。

▶ **語言陷阱 Language Traps:**

1. There is no difference between the two valves readings.
   兩個閥體的數據並無差異。
2. There are a lot of issues that come with the factory's making the changes without our approval first.
   工廠沒有我們的同意而任意做改變，帶來許多的問題。
3. Owner's manuals will have to be changed.
   使用手冊也要改。
4. Without the end customer's approval, this change could disqualify us as a supplier.
   沒有消費者的認可，我們可能變成不合格的供應商。
5. What did the factory do to qualify the new design?
   工廠做了什麼來保證新設計的品質？
6. What extra costs were incurred because of the change?
   因為這改變而多出來的成本是多少？
7. I will not accept the change.
   我不會接受更改。

▶ **技法字詞 Tricky Words and Phrases:**

installation and adjustment procedures 安裝跟調整步驟
owner's manuals 操作手冊
disqualify (v.) 不合格
incur (v.) 招致，惹起

● 新手任務 Your Mission:
我們將如何排除客戶的困難，才能讓客戶願意接受修改？

● 試寫Now You Try: 請試寫於下方

（試寫後才翻頁）

教戰守則 Insider Tips

　　客戶多出來的作業成本（更改給消費者的使用說明）無疑是最大考量，還可能因為修改設計讓他喪失經銷商的資格，我們多年的合作恐怕會功虧一簣。然而我們的修改也並非沒事找事，是為了產品更穩定，也為了彼此的長遠利益著想。

　　這個案子要解決，眼前的目標必須使任何一方都不會因為設計更動而賠錢，並且必須以客戶方不更動「使用者手冊」為原則來修改產品，這當然需要仰賴工程師的技術，但也是此時唯一讓客戶點頭的辦法。

▶ **語言祕訣 Language Tips:**

1. 表示理解及感激

We understand your rejection **and appreciate** that you let us know about your concerns.

我們理解你的拒絕，並且感謝你告訴我們你關心的問題。

2. 重申更改有利多

Our reason for this change is "to precisely adjust the pressure of the valve as required."

我們更改的理由是「按照要求，更精準地調整閥的壓力」。

3. 詢問接受其他可能

Will you accept only the change of the thread without adding the washer?

你可以接受只有把螺紋改變，而不放墊片嗎？

4. 告知解決方案

It will solve the problems you mentioned for rejection.

這樣會使你拒絕我們的問題消失。

5. **衷心請求認可**

We wholeheartedly await your approval.

我們全心等待你的認可。

▶ **關鍵字詞** Key Words and Phrases:

concerns (n.) 關心的問題

solve (v.) 解決

await (v.) 等待

💬 信件範例 Sample Letter:

我方發信給客戶 Our Email to the Client

Dear Robert,

We understand your rejection and appreciate that you let us know about your concerns. Our reason for this change, as mentioned in our previous mail, is "to precisely adjust the pressure of the valve as required."

Will you accept only the change of the thread from 6/10-12 UNC to 6/12-14 UNF without adding the washer? It will be helpful for our production. It will also solve the problems you mentioned for rejection.

Thank you and please advise any thoughts. We wholeheartedly await your approval.

Best regards,

Kelly

親愛的羅伯：

我們理解你的拒絕，並且感謝你告訴我們你關心的問題。我們更改的理由，如上封信所說，是「按照要求，更精準地調整閥的壓力」。

你可以接受只有把螺紋從6/10-12 UNC改成6/12-14 UNF，而不放墊片嗎？這樣對我們生產線很有幫助，也會使你拒絕我們的問題消失。

謝謝，請告訴我們任何的想法，我們全心等待你的認可。

誠摯祝福，

凱莉

🐎 客戶回覆 Client's Reply

Kelly,

Please send drawing of the thread change. Mark the location. I'll see what to do next.

Robert Jonson

凱莉：

請寄來螺紋更改的繪圖，標出位置，我會看下一步怎麼做。

羅伯強森

 客戶來信：重點解讀 Getting the Hidden Messages

客戶要求看工程繪圖，顯示有轉圜餘地了。

▶ 客戶用語表達 Client's Expressions:

1. Please send drawing of the thread change. Mark the location.
請寄來螺紋更改的繪圖，標出位置。

2. I'll see what to do next.
我會看下一步怎麼做。

▶ 技法字詞 Tricky Words and Phrases:

drawing (n.) 繪圖
mark (v.) 標記

Round 6
第六回合

 客戶回覆 Client's Reply

> Kelly,
>
> If the only change is the thread, as you said, then I'll approve the change.
>
> Usually the whole valve will be changed if high pressure is an issue. Throughout our company history we have not had a request for a complete valve change. For this reason, we can easily make a decision to accept your change and make thread as a spare part to be purchased in the future when needed.
>
> Robert Johnson

凱莉：

如果按你所說，只有螺紋的改變，那我可以同意這項更改。

通常高壓造成問題，整個閥要被換掉。從本公司的歷史來看，我

們還沒有碰到整個閥換掉的情形。因此，我們可以很容易做決定接受你們的更改，將來需要的話，再以零件來購買螺絲。

　　羅伯強森

客戶來信：重點解讀 Getting the Hidden Messages

　　我們為客戶設想的結果，終於讓客戶有條件同意修改了，客戶也告訴我們他同意的理由，有利我們更了解客戶狀況，作為將來密切合作的基礎。

▶ **客戶用語表達 Client's Expressions:**

1. If the only change is the thread, then I'll approve the change.
   如果只有螺紋的改變，我可以同意這項更改。

2. We can easily make a decision to accept your change.
   我們可以容易做決定接受你們的更改。

▶ **技法字詞 Tricky Words and Phrases:**

approve (v.) 同意

request (n.) 要求

spare part 零件

新手任務 Your Mission:

終於盼到客戶點頭了，請回信給客戶。

（試寫後才翻頁）

教戰守則 Insider Tips

謝謝客戶同意修改，讓他知道在這些來往溝通的時間之後，我們仍會努力按照原本訂單的時間出貨。

▶ 語言祕訣 Language Tips:

1. **感謝**

   Thanks for your approval!

   謝謝你同意！

2. **告知目標**

   Now we are heading for the production to catch your shipment date on your PO.

   現在我們要投入生產，好追上你的訂單日期。

▶ 關鍵字詞 Key Words and Phrases:

head for 前進，投入

catch (v.) 追，趕

PO (purchase order) 訂單

● 信件範例 Sample Letter:

我方回信 Our Reply to the Client

Robert,

　　This is great news! Thanks for your approval. Now we are heading for the production to catch your shipment date on your PO.

Thanks again and have a nice day!

Kelly

羅伯：

　　這真是好消息，謝謝你同意！現在我們要投入生產，好追上你的訂單日期。

　　再次感謝，並祝美好的一天！

　　凱莉

★★★★★★★★★★★★★★目標達成★★★★★★★★★★★★★★

客戶了解他沒有損失，而是增加福利之後，目標達成。

註：如果一開始我們的人員就了解要怎樣傳遞「恰當的」訊息給客戶，就能大大降低被客戶拒絕接受的風險。唯有適當的解釋，站在客戶立場，讓客戶了解他沒有損失，而是增加福利之後，目標才容易達成。

附錄
Appendixes

老闆的地雷句
The Responses That Tick Off Your Boss

主管讀完實習生給客戶寫的第一封信差點昏倒，為什麼？

Letter 1:

Dear Sandy,

Hi, I am Emma Chiu, Vicky's new assistant. If you have any questions, please ask me.

Below is the information of the three POs and the shipment dates...

Emma

信件一：

親愛的珊蒂：

嗨，我是艾瑪邱，薇琪的新助理，如果你有任何問題，請問我。

下面是你三張訂單的資訊以及出貨日期……

艾瑪

解析

對客戶一開始自我介紹就說「有任何問題，請來問我」，簡直是挖洞給自己跳。這是餐飲服務業以客為尊的制式臺詞，並不適用在貿易業。你的主管會希望你把精力放在解決真正的問題上，所以這樣熱血的字句應該放最後面，也就是說問題範圍不可包山包海，而要限制在那三張訂單的範圍，客戶對這些訂單有任何不清楚之處可問我們，才避免用錯精力又自找麻煩。

地雷句

×If you have any questions, please always let me know.

✓ 正確句

○If you have any questions about the three POs or the shipment dates, please let us know.

Letter 2:

Hello, Tony,

We are sorry to say that we cannot push the shipment prior to G20, but we will let you know if the shipment date can go sooner.

Thank You.

Jenny

信件二：

嗨，東尼：

我們很抱歉跟你說我們沒辦法在G20前出貨，但如果出貨日可以

早一些的話，我們會讓你知道。

謝謝！

珍妮

 解析

老闆希望業務回信時，能多想幾句，尤其是站在客戶的立場角度，想好了再回信，這就是孫子說的「慎戰」。

你對客戶直接說「不能」、「沒辦法」、「你錯了」，保證一秒惹毛主管，公司期待員工解決問題，不是來說「不」的，所以必須善盡「溝通」之責，擁有良好的處事與工作態度（努力、自信、誠信、負責、熱情、勇氣、毅力、關懷等），把不可能變成可能，方法用盡才可以說「恐怕有困難」。

 地雷句

✕ We are sorry to say that we cannot push the shipment prior to G20.

✓ 正確句

○ After negotiation, it is difficult to move the shipment forward before G20.

 其他地雷句

✕ 處理客訴問題：這是客人的錯，不是我們的錯。

✕ 我不知道該如何回覆，我不負責。

✕ 我們大學老師說的不是這樣。（如何變通與時俱進？）

✕ 我的主管（同事）不教我。（同事理所當然要教新人嗎？）

✕ 這好像很難，我不會，我可以做簡單點的嗎？

✕ 我若在其他地方工作，賺的錢比這裡多。（表示自己很委

屈？）

✕這客戶很難搞耶，又要來亂，我不想處理這客戶了。

✕我現在下班嘍，我想明天才回這信，反正是公司急，又不是我急。

✕這不是我的工作。

✕老闆為什麼我們要寫會議紀錄？為什麼不是對方寫？他們說英文，開會說英文嘛！

✕我不是樂觀的人，我不會這樣寫。

✕我有我的速度，你催我也快不了。

✕我的個性就是這樣，要不然你請別的同事回這封信。

✕我哪知道客戶想要的是什麼？

✕我們出差會去購物嗎？有時間去outlet嗎？要帶泳衣嗎？（自己帶就好，不要問）

✕老闆，你說我不夠用心，我覺得我很用心了，公司有看到嗎？

✕老闆，你說我不夠用心，這公司是我的嗎？

✕老闆，你早上說我做得很好，那我下個月可以加薪嗎？

✕客人覺得我們的員工腦袋有問題，因為員工寫了這樣的句子：

Taiwan is Taiwan. China is China. Made in Taiwan is Taiwan-Made. Made in China is China-made.

✕中國員工常說的話：

(1) 我們這裡就是這樣做。

(2) 這不是我的錯，以前就一直這樣做的。

地雷行為

自私行爲無論到哪裡都是不受歡迎的，公司期待新人成爲上駟之材，但不懂待人接物、應對進退，搞不清楚狀況，不知道自己的角色位置，沒禮貌又不知道自己無禮的情形，實不少見。離開學校進入職場，具劣勢特質、不積極改進的人自然不會有人願意教導，能力勢必無法提升，也無法通過試用期。

・一開口就得罪人，惹麻煩幫倒忙。

・每個人都「應該」教他／她、幫他／她。

・負面思考，導致負面溝通與行爲。

・傳播負面情緒（網路言行），影響他人。

・無敏感度及禮貌，直接撥內線給主管問問題，不管主管是否正在忙。

・女新人寫信要求到國外男客戶家當沙發客，公私不分與占便宜心態，不顧公司及社會觀感。

・助理陪同業務主管出國與客戶開會，沒有周詳的準備，只想著肥一己私心，利用出國機會完成個人願望。（無非故意踩主管紅線，還未與客戶交手就已經戰敗。既未達成目標，還浪費了出國可觀的經費及時間。）

 其他地雷句

1. 老闆：你怎麼可以回客人信只寫一句（Yes）？

   小白：老闆，你不是說簡單的回信就可以嗎？

2. 老闆：DD的客戶投訴你，說你常常給的資料東漏西漏。

   小白：是客人沒說清楚，我又不是他的蛔蟲。

3. 老闆：這是很低級的錯誤，你怎麼會犯錯，而且還犯了兩次錯！

   小白：我回座位罰寫一百遍，下次若有再錯就不能怪我喔！

4. 老闆：你跟印度客人開會的會議紀錄呢？

　小白：沒啥內容要向你報告的，就開會吃飯聊天，客人問一些我們公司的狀況。

5. 老闆：我覺得這樣寫得不夠好，不夠仔細，客戶會誤會你的意思，你再去修改一下。

　小白：不會啊！我覺得已經很好了！我也不知要如何修改。

　　新人初始工作能力不足，職場第一關必須從良好的工作態度開始（有禮貌、積極、認真、負責、合作、易溝通、好相處、尊重他人等），其他人才可能願意教導，新人也才能逐漸培養工作能力。與人溝通相處不外乎替人設想，才能有良好的溝通。

看懂溝通招術
Breaking Communication Gimmicks

　　為了爭取對自己有利的狀況，客戶可能使用各種花招或藉口，雖然我們心知肚明，但不要戳破，而是要看懂溝通招數，鬥而不破，四兩撥千金。

1. **電話牌**

　利用講電話的特性占優勢，客戶利用本身英語為母語或電話可能講不清楚的特性，創造有利於自己的狀況。破解之道為通話後，發出談話紀錄。

2. **旅遊牌**

　客戶打出旅遊牌的目的在於創造難以捉摸的情境，產生有利於自己的狀況。旅遊時客戶是否收發信我們不得而知，在客戶所稱旅遊期間，所有事情都是不確定的。客戶如果在旅遊時打電

話來或要我們打電話去，就是打雙重牌局。

3. **財務牌（會計牌，銀行牌）**

客戶延遲付款時，會說要問財務部，過兩天回信時，會說負責的會計休假，等幾天回來後再去銀行匯款，下封信說會去問銀行，總之，客戶經常輪流打財務、會計、銀行這三張牌，拖延付款時間。

4. **新人牌**

客戶打新人牌可能是真的，也可能是推延時間的說詞，無論是新助理或是新倉管，都需要時間摸索才能進入狀況。

5. **倉庫牌**

客戶可能有好幾個倉庫，可能歸不同的人管，問來問去時間就被拖掉了。

6. **零售顧客牌**

客戶想轉嫁成本打出零售顧客牌，要你吸收他的顧客成本。

7. **兜圈牌**

客戶不斷重複數落我方品質，讓你開始煩，而失去該有的戒心。

8. **好心牌**

客戶「好心的」告訴你，因為英文不是臺灣的母語，所以他寫了很長的解釋給你。

9. **亂湊牌**

將事實經過的時間順序亂湊，置入錯誤資訊，似是而非，如我方未及時糾正，可能蒙受重大損失。

10.詭字牌

客戶使用足以讓我們損失重大，但我們卻未必能在第一時間就察覺的弔詭文字，如rebate及所有合約用字。

11.共識牌

客戶將其一廂情願的想法，說成雙方有「共識」。

12.糖衣牌

客戶感謝你跟他的生意往來，接下來就提出降價或其他要你配合的要求。

13.煙幕牌

客戶緊咬我方品質有問題，害他要派人手檢查修理及處理後續，所以要扣款或是要下一批貨降價。

14.立即牌

客戶營造錯誤的立即感，但他所提出的時間與條件，真的立即嗎？

國際貿易進出口流程圖
International Trade Transaction Flow Chart

https://market.cloud.edu.tw/content/vocation/business/ks_sm/111.htm
（教育部教育雲、教育大市集）

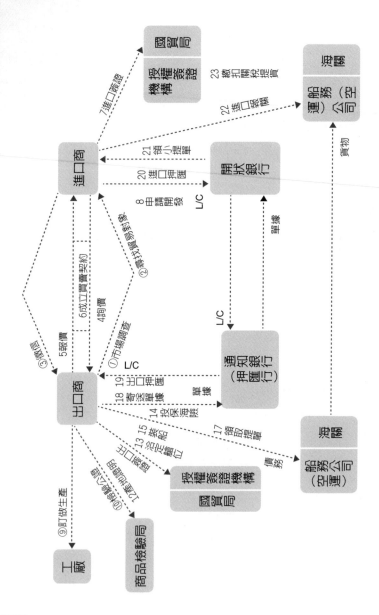

聯合國（電子化）貿易文件一覽表
The United Nations electronic Trade Documents (UNeDocs)

聯合國為便捷國際貿易，依使用情形將貿易文件分為以下九大類（資料來源——經濟部國貿局）：

1. **生產**（Production）
   - 訂購單（Purchase order）
   - 製造指示（Manufacturing instructions）
   - 物料供應（Stores requisition）
   - 商業發票資料單（Invoicing data sheet）
   - 裝箱單（Packing list）

2. **採購**（Purchase）
   - 詢價（Enquiry）
   - 意願書（Letter of intent）
   - 訂單（Order）
   - 運送指示（Delivery instructions）
   - 運送放行（Delivery release）

3. **銷售**（Sale）
   - 報價（Offer/Quotation）
   - 合約（Contract）
   - 訂單確認（Acknowledgement of order）
   - 發貨單（Proforma invoice）
   - 送貨通知（Dispatch order）
   - 商業發票（Commercial invoice）

4. 付款──銀行（Payment–Banking）
  · 銀行匯款通知（Instructions for bank transfer）
  · 收款單（Collection order）
  · 付款單（Payment order）
  · 押匯信用證申請（Documentary credit application）
  · 押匯信用證（Documentary credit）

5. 保險（Insurance）
  · 保險證明（Insurance certificate）
  · 保險單（Insurance policy）
  · 保險用發票（Insurer's invoice）
  · 承保單（Cover note）

6. 仲介服務（Intermediary services）
  · 運送指示（Forwarding instructions [FIATA-FFI]）
  · 承攬業通知出口商（Freight Forwarder's advice to exporter）
  · 承攬業收據證明（Forwarder's certificate of receipt [FIATA-FCR]）
  · 港口收費相關文件（Port charges documents）
  · 運送單（Delivery order）

7. 運輸（Transport）
  · 綜合運輸文件（Universal [multipurpose] transport document）
  · 海運提單（Sea waybill）
  · 提單（Bill of Lading）
  · 訂單確認（Booking confirmation）
  · 貨物到港通知（Arrival notice [goods]）

8. 出口規定（Exit regulations）
   · 輸出許可證申請（Export license application）
   · 輸出許可（Export license）
   · 貨物出口通關（Goods declaration for exportation）
   · 貨物報關（Cargo declaration）
   · 檢驗證明申請（Application for inspection certificate）

9. 進口及過境規定（Entry and transit regulations）
   · 輸入許可證申請（Import license, application）
   · 輸入許可證（Import license）
   · 外匯許可（Foreign exchange permit）
   · 家用物品通關（Goods declaration for home use）
   · 海關貨物即時放行（Customs immediate release declaration）

經貿資訊站
Business-Related Websites

▶ 臺灣

1. **中華民國對外貿易發展協會**Taiwan External Trade Development Council（TAITRA）—— **全球資訊網**（Global Trade Source）
   http://www.taitraesource.com
   可查詢168國各國基本資料、主要產業狀況、市場投資環境、與我國經貿關係、當地商展活動等。

2. **臺灣經貿網**（Taiwantrade）
   https://info.taiwantrade.com
   提供焦點商情活動、商機撮合、全球採購網、發燒議題、網路

安全詐騙實例、貿易百寶箱等資訊。

3. **經濟部國際貿易局（Bureau of Foreign Trade）經貿資訊網**

   https://www.trade.gov.tw

   經濟部國貿局負責掌理我國國際貿易政策之研擬、貿易推廣及進出口管理事項，提供會展資訊、線上申辦表格，查詢貿易法規或政策，並提供每日全球商情等訊息。

▶ 中國

1. **江蘇外貿論壇**

   http://bbs.jsiec.cn

   中國外貿人氣網站，提供交流互動討論與商務及其他外貿相關討論區，如：外貿業務交流區、國外採購商資料區、外貿知識學習區、外貿生活感受區、產品推薦、展會訊息、貨運物流、涉外法律等。

2. **福步外貿論壇（FOB Business Forum）**

   http://bbs.fobshanghai.com

   中國外貿人氣網站，提供外貿業務、外貿區域市場、外貿行業交流、電子商務、外貿經理人、外貿配套服務、外貿急診室等交流。

3. **跨國外貿論壇（Global Importer）**

   http://bbs.globalimporter.net

   中國外貿人氣網站，提供綜合交流、外貿問答、外貿展會、外貿新聞、商務中心、外貿博客（部落格）等訊息。

4. **合眾外貿論壇**

   http://fob107.com

   中國外貿人氣網站，提供進／出口論壇、外貿展會、電子商務、外貿防騙、世界各國習俗禮儀等討論區。

5. **阿里巴巴商友圈（1688.com）**

   http://club.1688.com

   中國外貿人氣網站，提供論壇、生意經、商友圈、博客（部落格）等資訊。

國家圖書館出版品預行編目資料

國際商務英語：溝通策略與運用／黃靜悅著.
－－初版. －－臺北市：五南, 2018.03
　面；　公分
ISBN 978-957-11-9039-6 (平裝)

1.商業英文　2.讀本

805.18　　　　　　　　　　106000823

1X0D

國際商務英語：溝通策略與運用

作　　者 — 黃靜悅（291.4）

發 行 人 — 楊榮川

總 經 理 — 楊士清

副總編輯 — 黃文瓊

主　　編 — 朱曉蘋

責任編輯 — 吳雨潔　黃懷萱

封面設計 — 陳翰陞　謝瑩君

出 版 者 — 五南圖書出版股份有限公司

地　　址：106台北市大安區和平東路二段339號4樓

電　　話：(02)2705-5066　　傳　　真：(02)2706-6100

網　　址：http://www.wunan.com.tw

電子郵件：wunan@wunan.com.tw

劃撥帳號：01068953

戶　　名：五南圖書出版股份有限公司

法律顧問　林勝安律師事務所　林勝安律師

出版日期　2018年3月初版一刷

定　　價　新臺幣490元